With Our Bellies Full and the Fire Dying

Tales of Sinning and Redemption

Debra H. Goldstein

A bad meal is a misdemeanor but going to bed hungry is the biggest crime of all.

Ten short story authors have joined forces to write humorous crime stories containing some of their favorite Thanksgiving dishes. From murder to theft to bank heists, these authors have whipped up stories to tickle your funny bone, feed your urge for a good crime and make you a bit hungry in the process. Not to be outdone, Lisa Lynn provides the perfect accompaniment with recipes that people can make for the holidays using the basic staples found in nearly every home or from your local food bank.

Thanks to the publisher's "Misti Gives Back" program, 100% of the net proceeds of the sales of this title will be split evenly among each of the contributors' local Second Harvest Food Bank (a member of Feeding America) to help raise money to feed those most in need and at risk. If a contributor does not have a Second Harvest in their area, their share will go directly to Feeding America. Your purchase(s) ensure that more people will have access to food this holiday season and beyond.

Please visit Feeding America to learn more about food insecurity and how you can help in your local area.

Features fiction from *Sandra Murphy, Heidi Hunter, Jim Fusilli, Barry Ergang, Linda K. Hardie, Debra H. Goldstein, Nikki Knight, Daniel Sohn, Lesley A. Diehl, Shari Held and Lisa Lynn*

Available from
https://whitecitypress.com/product/the-perp-wore-pumpkin-edited-by-j-alan-hartman/

With Our Bellies Full
and the Fire Dying
Tales of Sinning and Redemption
Debra H. Goldstein

Published by White City Press

An imprint of Misti Media LLC

https://whitecitypress.com

Available in both Paperback and eBook Editions

1 2 3 4 5 6 7 8 9 10

Copyright © Debra H. Goldstein 2025

Paperback ISBN: 9781963479683

eBook ISBN: 9781963479676

The following works have previously appeared in:

Thanksgiving in Moderation — *The Killer Wore Cranberry: a Fourth Meal of Mayhem* (Untreed Reads—October 2014)

Pig Lickin' Good — *Parnell Hall Presents Malice Domestic: Mystery Most Edible* (2019)

Who Dat? Dat the Indian Chief! — *Mardi Gras Murder* (Mystery & Horror, LLC—2014)

Wabbit's Carat — *Bethlehem Writers Roundtable* (January 2021)

The Girls in Cabin Three — *Black Cat Mystery Magazine*, Vol. 12 (August 2022)

A Political Cornucopia — *Bethlehem Writers Roundtable* (November 2013)

Violet Eyes — *OMDB!* (Dec 2015)]

The Rabbi's Wife Stayed Home — *Mysterical-E* (April 2014)]

The Night They Burned Ms. Dixie's Place — *Alfred Hitchcock Mystery Magazine* (May/June 2017)

So Beautiful or So What — *Paranoia Blues: Crime Fiction Inspired by the Songs of Paul Simon* (2022)

Bucket List Dreams — *Murder by the Glass: Cocktail Mysteries* (Untreed Reads 2021)

Harvey and the Redhead — *The Eyes of Texas: Private Eyes from the Panhandle to the Piney Woods* (Down & Out Books—October 2019)

Biff's Place — *Jukes & Tonks: Crime Music Inspired by Music in the Dark and Suspect Choices* (Down & Out Books- 2021)

Grandma's Garden — www.Alalit.com (2014)

Forensic Magic — *Masthead: Best New England Crime Stories* (Level Best Books—Dec 2020)

A Corn Puddin' Wedding — *Kings River Life Magazine* (Nov 2016)

Legal Magic 01— www.Alalit.com (2011)

This Is Where I Buried My Wives — *Bethlehem Writers Roundtable* (Sept/Oct 2015)

Contents

Introduction

In life, we all tend to have moments where we give thanks for wonderful things that happen, times we ask forgiveness or redemption for wrongs we have committed, and occasions we simply shut our eyes and sin. This collection of short stories strives to capture these instances in ways that entertain readers. Enjoy!

Thanksgiving in Moderation

Thanksgiving is a holiday that brings out the best and the worst in families!

Thanksgiving always has been a good time for weddings—especially second and third or in this case, the fifth time around. Alicia, my sister, gladly ticked the benefits of a Thanksgiving Day wedding off on her fingers each time for my mother and me. "One, the entire family already is together so I won't get stuck buying extra plane tickets for my fiancé's or own kids; two, nobody can complain about what I serve because the turkey, dressing, greens, yams, and pumpkin pie menu is set, plus I save money because everyone brings a dish; and, three, my husband never has an excuse to forget our anniversary because no matter what the actual date of our wedding is, we'll always celebrate it on Thanksgiving Day."

Somewhere between numbers two and three, our now eighty-five-year-old mother, who often lacks a filter, suggested Alicia would be better off sleeping with the men she dates rather than marrying them. Unfortunately, Alicia believes that living together without benefit of holy matrimony, like Bob and I do, is a mortal sin. I bet all three of her surviving ex-spouses raise a glass to her every Thanksgiving.

Eleven years ago, Paul, her first husband, had a massive coronary and left her with eight-year-old twin girls and a small fortune. Up to now, as her legal advisor, I've managed to protect her by insisting she have each would-be hubby sign a prenuptial agreement with a gigolo clause. The gigolo clause gives a husband who lasts one day over three years a flat $100,000 if there are divorce proceedings. The three stooges, as I refer to Harry, Larry and Carlos, each fled Alicia days after becoming eligible for their $100,000 payoffs.

Tonight, after we eat Alicia's daughter's pumpkin pie, Alicia plans to make Philippe her fifth husband. She giggles and blushes whenever he whispers "Je t'aime" or other French tidbits into her ear. I snicker. French with a Mississippi accent is a bit difficult for me to swallow. Somehow "moan cherry" doesn't do it for me like it does for Alicia.

I'm also finding it difficult to swallow the fact that this time she's refusing to let me draft a prenuptial agreement. She keeps telling me, "Philippe is my perfect soul mate. We'll be together forever and a day."

Maybe I'm a cynic, but I'm not as optimistic as Alicia. The private detective I hired reported that Philippe or actually Philip West walked out of his Mississippi delta home one night twenty years ago to buy cigarettes and never came home to his wife and toddler daughter. They divorced and he opened a small antiques store in Jackson, Mississippi. According to my detective, West remarried once, but that wife died from injuries sustained in a fall at the antique store. Because they had no children and she had no other family, he was her only heir.

His adult daughter is here tonight to celebrate Thanksgiving and the wedding nuptials. They reconnected this past year when he reached out to her just before he had surgery to replace a leaky heart valve with a pig valve. The time of his surgery is also when Philippe and Alicia met.

Alicia volunteers one day a week as a pink lady on the cardiology wing she donated in memory of Paul. Last year, she was pushing a magazine cart to the different patient rooms a week after Carlos was granted his divorce. One of the rooms she visited was Philippe's. They clicked. Finding out he would be going home to an empty apartment, she insisted he move into her home where she could tend to his needs. Apparently, he liked her hovering. Other than to pick up his clothes, he never went back to his apartment.

When Paul, her first husband, was alive, our extended family celebrated Thanksgiving Norman Rockwell style at their house. Paul fried a turkey, Mom made a yam casserole smothered in marshmallows that was to die for, Alicia and her daughters made the desserts, and if I do say so myself, I did a pretty good job on the greens. After Paul died, things got a bit funky. We moved the dinner to my house and Mom, Bob, and I assumed most of the cooking responsibilities.

None of us are too happy about this wedding, but we've been working together to prepare an over-abundant Thanksgiving and wedding feast. At Mom's insistence, we added another ham and turkey breast to accommodate Philippe's seemingly insatiable appetite. Besides showing her concern about how much food we're going to need, Mom repeatedly has tried to reason with Alicia. From, "you have my blessing to simply live with him" to "Why be trussed like a turkey to a man closer in age to me than you?"

Alicia's daughters and Bob also expressed their doubts and tried to rein her in, but she refuses to listen to anyone except Philippe. He's been gung ho for a wedding almost from before he got out of the hospital.

I've done everything I can think of to slow down their wedding plans, but without any success. Out of desperation, I even attempted to build a friendship with Philippe by bringing him lunch for the past six months during my sister's weekly hairdresser appointment.

My sister would have her own heart attack if she realized that instead of quinoa, chicken, and vegetables, I've been feeding him well-seasoned steak, all my greens recipes trimmed out with bacon or pork, and the other things prohibited by his post-heart procedure diet. Bless his heart, he loves my food, but he won't reconsider signing a pre-nuptial agreement even with a sweetened dangling $200,000 clause.

So, I've given in and decorated my house for Thanksgiving and their wedding. Although nobody is thrilled, the family cooks are trying, for Alicia's sake, to make this a special Thanksgiving meal. As Mom suggested, when her efforts at logic failed, we owe it to Alicia and Philippe to each make a killer Thanksgiving dish.

Some people, like Alicia's daughter, Sarah, can bake up a storm for Thanksgiving desserts while others are known for making a specialty item like Paul's fried turkey. I'm the family's greens queen. A greens dish can be made with any leafy vegetable. Some of my favorites include spinach, kale, collards, cabbage, broccoli, brussel sprouts, and parsley. At some point during Philippe's recovery, I served him all of these things in my different recipes. Tonight, I'm introducing a new béchamel and greens dish at our almost extended family Thanksgiving dinner.

We've gathered around my equally extended dining room table. Besides all of my leaves, I've added two card tables so we can sit together. I evened out the various tabletops by putting some of my favorite mystery books by Carolyn Hart, Margaret Truman, Kaye George, and Alan Bradley under the extra tables' legs. Depending upon their publisher, a given author's books tend to be about the same amount of pages so by mixing them, I got a perfect table height.

Bob normally sits at the head of the table while I take the other end seat so I can get in and out to replenish our family style platters, but Philippe, with a few glasses of wine under his belt, usurped my chair. His daughter had left him a seat between Alicia and her, but when he ignored it while she was getting him a wine refill, she quietly moved to the one closer to Alicia. I slid into her vacated seat as she leaned over to put another full glass of wine in front of her father.

At Bob's request we joined hands for a prayer of Thanksgiving, but Philippe broke the chain because he was too busy whispering something to Alicia and holding her hand under the table as if we couldn't see what they were doing. Based on her giggling, he must have been whispering in French. Bob got as far as "Heavenly Father," when his youngest granddaughter, Betty, jumped up, almost knocking her water glass over.

"I learned a new Thanksgiving prayer!" Getting a nod of approval from Bob, Betty proudly shouted: "Rub a dub dub, and thanks for the grub."

We barely said "Amen" before we stabbed serving forks and spoons into the mounds of food on the table. I couldn't help but picture us as naked vultures swooping and diving up and down over the table—especially when two of the adults almost got into a fistfight over who grabbed the wishbone first.

I was pleased to see everyone except little Betty, who declared my greens to be "smelly," taste them. Philippe loaded his plate high with my béchamel and greens. Between bites, he said, "You've got to share this recipe with Alicia. It's delicious." He took a swig of wine, even though Alicia made one of her disapproving faces.

"Oh, it's very simple, you can use chard, kale or spinach as your base, but I chose kale and some accent parsley from the greens we grow out back in our organic garden. Of course, I had to wash the slugs off first," I said. "Slugs are pretty slippery things, but I think I got all of them."

My mother and Alicia put their forks down on the tablecloth. Philippe kept eating. "I coarsely chopped the greens and stems, steamed them until cooked through, and then squeezed them dry in cheesecloth. This really is a simple recipe. Alicia, even you could make it for Philippe."

"I can't wait," she said, turning toward Philippe. As he picked up his wineglass, she quietly asked, "Don't you think you've had enough greens and wine? She turned toward me. "He's still taking a blood thinner so his cardiologist wants him to do things in moderation."

Philippe winked at me. "This is a holiday. I can be moderate tomorrow." He pawed at Alicia's hand again while he used his free hand to shake extra salt over his second helping of greens. It was nice to see him eat with such gusto.

Years ago the ratio of time and effort I put into preparing our Thanksgiving dinner against the time it took my family and friends to devour it bothered me, but I learned to accept the fact that we make a pretty darn good meal. The smiles as everyone polished off dinner and the compliments I received on my greens felt rewarding. For a minute, but only a minute, as I began to clear, I forgot about the impending nuptials.

My mother and little Betty immediately rose to help. We quickly established a system of them bringing the dishes from the dining room to the kitchen while I scraped and emptied any food remnants down the garbage disposal before loading my dishwasher. Our efficient clean-up done, I sent my helpers back into the dining room with plates and forks for dessert. Pausing only to turn on the dishwasher, I followed them back into the dining room with the pies Alicia's daughter Sarah had made.

"Pecan pie, please," Bob said.

Not to be outdone, six-year-old Betty piped up, "Pumpkin." As I sliced a small piece for her, she said: "I learned a new song for Thanksgiving at school. Do you want to hear it?" Without waiting for an answer, Betty launched into a rendition of "America the Beautiful."

Philippe stared at the sliver of pumpkin pie being passed to Betty, who still was busy singing. "I need a bigger piece than that," he said to me. I glanced at Alicia who shrugged and mouthed the word moderation. Ignoring her, I cut him a chunk of pumpkin pie. He was halfway through it before I served everyone else.

"Some adults have no manners," my mother mumbled. I almost didn't hear her over Betty's shouting of the chorus, especially when all the pumpkin pie eaters, except Philippe, began gagging and grabbing their goblets of water or wine.

I took a bite of the pumpkin pie and spit it back on my plate. "Sarah," I sputtered, after swallowing some water. "You used salt instead of sugar!"

Tears welled in her eyes. "I don't know how that happened," she said. Before I could reply, there was a noise from Philippe's end of the table. I looked toward the noise and was surprised to see Philippe standing and shaking, clutching the table to stay upright.

Alicia reached toward him. "Philippe, are you okay?" Philippe turned his head in the direction of Alicia's voice, but I could see his eyes weren't focusing on her. Alicia and I both rose from our seats. Philippe fell to the floor convulsing and gasping for air.

I felt for a pulse as Alicia cradled Philippe's head and everyone else sat stunned. I yelled over my shoulder "Call 911." One of Alicia's daughters whipped out her cellphone, dialed and then looked up to ask the address of the house.

By now, Bob knelt on the floor with me, trying to pry Alicia away from Philippe so we could turn him over and administer CPR. From the floor, I grabbed the napkin Philippe had dropped and wiped away the white foam coming from his mouth. Then, I bent his head back and began CPR chest compressions. I processed the sound of my mother taking Betty from the dining room still singing and of people letting the paramedics in, but I kept my attention focused on pushing on Philippe's still flat chest.

Time blurred as the paramedics started an IV and someone declared Philippe gone. I can't remember if they took him away or if the detective came first. All I know is I cleared the dessert dishes and then found myself in the living room with the rest of the shell-shocked guests not believing what had transpired.

"He seemed fine during dinner," Mom said. "He ate like a pig."

"Probably a result of his new heart valve." I laughed. I couldn't help myself.

"He's dead because of me," Philippe's daughter said. She walked over to the bar and poured herself a glass of scotch. "He told me he wasn't supposed to drink, except in moderation, and I kept his wine glass filled throughout dinner."

"Don't flatter yourself," my mom replied. "You might have helped him have a headache tomorrow, but you didn't kill him."

"But his meds and the wine."

"Unless he was an alcoholic…" the detective began.

"Oh, he wasn't," Alicia interjected. She sat down on the loveseat, unable to hold back her tears.

"Then, one night of overdoing it didn't kill him," the detective said.

Sarah walked over to sit on the couch next to Alicia. She covered her mother's hand with her own, but looked up at the detective. "I'm the guilty party. I didn't want my mother to waste her time or her money marrying such a jerk so I killed him by putting salt in my pumpkin pie instead of sugar."

I must have sucked my breath in and made a sound because Sarah glanced at me. "You know I'm too good a baker to make that kind of stupid mistake." She turned back toward the detective. "I knew he was on a low salt diet, so I made sure he had way too much salt today and would retain fluid." She held out her hands to be handcuffed.

The detective let out a groan, but kept a straight face. "One day of retaining fluid and breaking his low salt diet wouldn't have killed him any more than one day of not drinking in moderation. You may have contributed to whatever happened, but neither of you," he said, pointing at Philippe's daughter who was raiding my bar without any thought of moderation, "caused his death."

The detective turned to ask another question of all of us, but little Betty planted herself in front of him. He bent down to her level. "Don't tell me you're going to confess, too?"

"What's confess? I just wanted to tell you Mr. Philippe ate the smelly greens." The detective glanced around the room.

I waved at him. "She's talking about a new béchamel and greens dish I served. It was for everyone, but especially for him because he's always loved my greens," I noticed the detective's jaw tighten, so I hastened to add, "I ate a large portion of my greens as did most of the guests except Betty."

"Would you like me to sing my new song again," Betty asked the detective.

"No," my mother said. She took Betty by the hand and started toward the kitchen, but turned back to the detective and pulled herself to the top of her five foot two inch height. "You're wasting your time. None of us was particularly fond of the man." Alicia stirred but mother stared her down. "Well, most of us weren't fond of the man and weren't thrilled my foolish daughter was going to marry him, but we didn't kill him."

The detective and I followed mother and Betty into the kitchen. The dishwasher was humming. Other than the stacked dessert plates and dirty glasses, nothing was out of place. "How can you have had Thanksgiving dinner and everything be so cleaned up?"

"We worked as a team."

"And does the team know how Philippe or Philip West died?"

"Of course," mom said. "The glutton killed himself." The detective waited for mother to continue. "I've taken a blood thinner for years and whether he was taking Coumadin, Plavix, aspirin or whatever after receiving his new valve, his doctors would have made it clear that he needed to minimize his salt, alcohol, and leafy green intake. He wouldn't have had enough today to harm him, but he's been pigging out since he got his pig part. So, I think he's to blame for his own death."

"We won't have the autopsy results for a few weeks, but I'm inclined to agree with you." He looked at his watch. "I think, if I hurry, I can make it to my daughter's house for Thanksgiving dinner."

"You do that," Mom said. "Have a happy Thanksgiving." I started to show him to the door, but mother rested her hand on my arm. "Betty will show him out." Once we heard the front door close, my mother turned toward me. "It didn't happen tonight, but I must say the final timing of the cumulative effect of all those green dishes you've been making for him was most convenient."

I didn't respond. I stared back at Mom, but didn't dare say a word. "I'm thankful how this Thanksgiving played out," she said, "But remember, I believe in moderation, can live without greens, and read the fine print on the drug handouts I get with my prescriptions."

* * *

Thanksgiving in Moderation *was included by Untreed Reads in* The Killer Wore Cranberry: a Fourth Meal of Mayhem *short story anthology in October 2014.*

Pig Lickin' Good

Pig Lickin' cake is a traditional Southern treat. Mama's were always a huge hit at the annual fundraiser, even if the making of them brought back memories of a tragedy...

My mama knew how to make a cake. You could guarantee if there was a church bazaar or potluck where desserts were going to be auctioned off, Father Horst would stop by our house a few weeks ahead of time to ask Mama to donate two of her cakes. Normally, he didn't care what kind of cakes Mama made, but for the annual Ladies Auxiliary Fourth of July Potluck fundraiser, he'd come, hat in hand, sweet talking her to bake two of her Pig Lickin' cakes. He'd tell her there wasn't anyone else in the whole county who made a cake as light and moist as her Mandarin orange specialty.

Even though she hated the ladies of the auxiliary, she'd do anything for him—even breaking the promise she made every year to never make another Pig Lickin' cake. According to Mama, she owed him. Father Horst was the only one who spoke up and said Daddy shouldn't be on death row.

Not that it had made a difference. Everyone from around here, 'cept Mama and Father Horst, knew it was an open and shut case. After all, they had a dead man, a suspect standing over the body, and a bloody knife pried from Daddy's left hand. The jury wasn't even out for an hour before it came back with its guilty verdict. It was clear to the jurors that Daddy had killed Judd Brown.

The first few times we went to church after the trial, we sat in the same center pew we always had. Mama stared straight ahead, but I saw the ladies of the auxiliary point at us and I heard their whispers. They thought an eight-year-old was too young to understand what they were saying, but I wasn't. That's how I learned the details of Daddy's trial, and that while nobody was particularly sorry Judd Brown was dead, they sure pitied Mama and me.

On the Sunday right after the hearing, instead of listening to Father Horst's sermon, Ms. Ida and Ms. Mae, the president and vice-president of the auxiliary, whispered in hushed tones to anyone who hadn't crowded into the courtroom about how they testified, hand on the Bible. They wanted everyone to know that the last day Judd Brown took a breath on this earth, they walked into the church's kitchen and saw Judd lying on the ground with Daddy bent over him. Daddy's left hand was curled around the handle of the knife stuck in Judd's chest. He used his right hand to wave them back.

Even though Ms. Ida kept her voice low, I heard every word she said. "I screamed! He turned and stared at me with the coldest eyes I've ever seen. Even now, if I shut my eyes, I can still see those—hard and cold pieces of coal twinkling with the brilliance of a diamond."

I squeezed my eyes as tightly closed as I could, but the only eyes that came into my mind were soft brown ones that matched my cocker spaniel's.

The year after Daddy went away, after Father Horst came by the house before the Fourth of July Potluck, Mama started letting me help her make her Pig Lickin' cakes. My job, like Daddy's used to be when he helped her, was gathering up the ingredients to make the second cake. I got a yellow cake mix, can of mandarin oranges, vanilla pudding mix, powdered sugar, vanilla extract, and a can of crushed pineapple out of the pantry. The margarine, four eggs, and Cool Whip came from our refrigerator.

Once I placed the ingredients on the table, I kept quiet so instead of sending me out to play, she'd let me watch her add the cake mix, stick of softened margarine, teaspoon of vanilla extract, and half cup of the orange syrup drained from the canned oranges into the bowl of her electric mixer. After she mixed everything on medium-high for four minutes, she declared the mix to be well-blended. I didn't know about that, but it sure looked real light and fluffy before she dumped the drained oranges into the bowl. She mixed those up, too, until they broke into itty bitty pieces.

Satisfied, she tipped the mixer back and poured the batter from the bowl into a nine-by-thirteen pan and put it into the oven at 350 degrees. After she set a timer for thirty minutes, she returned to where I waited near the mixer.

When she said "Go," we each reached for a beater to lick clean. It felt a little funny. For the first time since I'd ever played the beater game, Daddy wasn't there jostling me before he let me grab the right beater.

As the years went by, Mama and I fell into a pattern of making the cakes together and then I'd deliver them to the church. I think Ms. Mae, still a fixture of the Ladies Auxiliary, must have forgotten who I was because whenever she told the story of her day in court, she stopped whispering around me.

I heard her tale so many times I got so I could predict when she was going to pause and pull out her hanky, monogrammed with its big *M*, to dab her eyes. After her silent moment, she'd look at whoever was listening and tell them how she cried on the stand as she explained to the jury how she screamed when Daddy yanked the cake knife out of Judd's chest. "He held it in his hand. We weren't going to wait and see what he did with it. Ida and I ran from that kitchen. We were plumb afraid he was going to use that knife on us. It's a miracle he didn't follow us."

He didn't. He simply stood there according to our police chief's testimony that I read in a copy of the trial transcript Mama left on the kitchen counter one night. I guess she'd been trying to write something to convince the governor not to electrocute Daddy. Usually, she worked on things to save Daddy only when I went to bed or wasn't home, but I guess something had distracted her and she forgot to put the transcript up. What with the date set for Daddy's electrocution and me getting ready to graduate high school and move on to Mississippi State, she might have forgotten to make the Pig Lickin' cakes if Father Horst hadn't reminded her about them when he made a special trip to our house to pick up the letter to the governor.

She couldn't say no to the good father, but for the first time that day, after the cake cooled and I washed the mixing bowl and beaters, Mama let me make the icing. Under her watchful eye, I carefully drained the can of pineapple, putting its liquid aside. I put the vanilla pudding mix in my clean mixing bowl, poured the pineapple juice onto it, and added half a cup of powdered sugar. I ran the mixer until all my ingredients were combined. Then, I whipped in about half a carton of the Cool Whip that had softened in the refrigerator. Once everything looked fluffy, I stirred in the drained crushed pineapple.

Mama ran her index finger over her beater. When she plopped her finger into her mouth, the shine of the wedding ring she still wore caught my eye.

"Perfect. I think the cake is cool, so you can turn it over onto the white platter and then spread the icing onto it."

I kept silent. Mama wasn't done talking.

"Don't forget to cover the sides. You wouldn't believe how many people forget to cover an entire cake."

I nodded. I'd seen plenty of cakes at the church bazaars that were heavy on icing on the top but barely touched on the sides.

"Once you spread that icing evenly, put the cakes in the refrigerator until you take them to the church tomorrow. I'm going to bed. I'm tired." She kissed my head and left me with the two cakes to ice and the transcript sitting on the counter to read.

The police chief's testimony was straightforward. "I pulled my gun before I walked into the kitchen in case he went crazy on us like Ida and Mae seemed to think he would, but he simply stood between the kitchen counter and where Judd lay. He still was holding that big cake knife in his left hand. I told him to drop it. He stared at me for a second before he let the knife fall from his fingers and held his hands out toward me. I guess he thought I'd handcuff him immediately. Instead, I kept my gun pointed at him while my deputy bagged the knife. Once my deputy was beyond his reach, I holstered my gun and cuffed him. He came peacefully with me."

After Daddy was sent to meet his maker, Mama hid the transcript in a drawer with a lock of his hair, a picture of the two of them and a very young Father Horst cutting up when the three might have been in high school, and a picture someone snapped of a more serious Father Horst marrying Mama and Daddy. Because nothing in that drawer ever moved between the times I looked through it, I decided Mama never opened the drawer. That's why, the year I went to law school, I took the Pig Lickin' cake recipe she'd written out and the transcript from the drawer with me. I don't know what I hoped to do with the transcript, but I thought having it might help me find answers to the many questions running around inside my head.

In law school, I was taught never to ask a question in a courtroom if I didn't already know the answer to it. My instructor used the example of a man accused of biting off the nose of the man he was fighting with. A witness had identified the lawyer's client. The lawyer asked, "Did you see my client bite off the plaintiff's nose?"

"No, sir," the witness answered.

Triumphantly, the lawyer postured for the entire courtroom. "Then, how can you say my client is the guilty party?"

"Because I saw him spit it out."

I guess Daddy's court-appointed lawyer missed that lesson because he asked the police chief, "How can you say my client is guilty?"

The police chief's answer was short and sweet. "The icing on his fingers."

"Icing?"

"Yes. There was a Pig Lickin' cake sitting on the counter. I guess he tried to cut himself a piece with the knife before he ended up using it on Judd."

"What makes you so sure he'd used the knife?"

"There was an indentation in the icing of the cake and icing on both the defendant's hand and the knife. There wasn't icing anywhere else in the kitchen except on the cake itself."

The transcript reported a laugh, but I don't know if it was the police chief reacting to his joke or from the courtroom audience chuckling. It didn't matter; the jury agreed the icing on his fingers and knife was enough evidence for Daddy's conviction. Still, something gnawed at me whenever I made and brought one of those easy-to-make Pig Lickin' cakes to a potluck or a party.

I'd take my finished cake from the refrigerator, cut it in squares, and at the last minute carefully place a mandarin orange on top of each square exactly like I'd done before I took Mama's cakes to the church. I had to be careful not to graze the top of the cake as I placed the oranges on each piece to avoid messing up the icing.

That's when it probably hit me, but I didn't put it all together until I came home for Mama's funeral after Father Horst called me at my New York law office to tell me she'd died unexpectedly. Crazed by the empty house, I made two Pig Lickin' cakes for the coffee and cake reception that was going to be held after her memorial service.

Father Horst came by the house to pay his respects the night before the funeral. He followed me into the kitchen after I offered to make him a cup of coffee. When I reached into the refrigerator for milk, he saw the iced cakes.

"They're for the reception. I had to make something."

"Those are perfect. I'm going back to the church when I leave here. Would you like me to put them in the fellowship hall refrigerator for you?"

"That would be most kind, but do you have the time to wait while I top each square with a mandarin orange?"

"No problem." He took the milk container from me, poured some into his coffee, and handed the container back to me. While it was still hot, he picked up the mug and turned its handle away from where I stood to his left. My eyes rested on his hands while he continued talking until I had to concentrate on putting the mandarin slices on each piece of cake without getting icing on my hand.

"I'm going to miss your mother. You know, your daddy and she were my friends long before they ever got married. Why, if she hadn't had eyes only for him, I might not have taken my vows and could have ended up being your daddy."

I kept my lips pressed together.

Father Horst smiled as he leaned forward, giving his lips a little lick.

"Know what I'm going to miss the most?"

"No, sir. I don't."

He pointed toward where I was placing mandarin orange slices on the last few cake squares. "Her Pig Lickin' cakes."

"But she only made those once a year." I glanced at my hand. As much as I'd tried to be careful, I'd still gotten a little icing on it.

"Not until..." his voice trailed off. When he spoke again, he'd moved on to a slight variation of his topic. "Of all her cakes, these were always my favorite. I used to run the bidding up on them during the church's silent auction until I could guarantee winning one of them. I'd pay for it and while everyone was busy eating, I'd slip away from the social hall to take my cake to the rectory. I wasn't going to share it with anyone."

He laughed. "I confess and hope you'll absolve me of my guilt about loving your mother's Pig Lickin' cakes."

"And should I absolve you of loving her so much you let an innocent man be put to death?"

Father Horst moved away from me. "I don't understand."

"But I do." I held up my right hand which still had traces of icing on it. I got up and walked toward the sink. Deliberately, I washed my hands and dried them with a dishtowel. Turning back, I met his gaze.

"Daddy was right-handed like me, but the police chief mentioned Daddy's left hand when he testified about the icing and the knife. If Daddy tasted the icing or put an orange on the cake, he would have instinctively used his right hand, so the icing would have been on his right hand like it was on mine. That means he intentionally got icing on his left hand."

Father Horst narrowed his eyes, so I could barely see his pupils. "You're not making sense. We all unconsciously use different hands to do different things depending upon how we're standing."

"When you pointed, took the milk container from me, or poured milk into your coffee, you used your dominant right hand. You even turned the coffee mug so you could hold its handle with your right hand. That's what we do unconsciously. Mama was a lefty. That's why she always grabbed the left mixing bowl beater while Daddy and I fought over the right one. She would have gotten icing on her left hand while putting the last touches on the cake. From the things I've heard about Judd Brown's lewd behavior, you probably know why she stabbed him, but that doesn't matter anymore. I gather when she came to you to confess, she told you something like Daddy came in, sized up the situation, sent her from the room, and grabbed the knife with his left hand to make it look like he was the one who'd killed Judd."

Father Horst stood silently in front of me, his mouth clenched tightly.

"Did you love her so much you wouldn't turn her in?"

"No, I loved God and my vows more than her. I took a vow of confidentiality, respecting matters heard in confession. I couldn't convince her to go against the agreement to be silent she'd made with your father, but I spoke out on his behalf and against capital punishment."

Now it was my turn to be confused. "But you tormented her by coming around every Fourth of July for those blasted Pig Lickin' cakes. That's a strange way to show you love someone."

"You misunderstand. That was my way of showing God's love for your mother. Her penance was having to make two Pig Lickin' cakes on each anniversary of the murder. I simply helped give her an avenue through which to make her act of penance."

He reached for my hand, but I shook him away. I got through the service and returned to New York that night. The first thing I did was tear up the Pig Lickin' cake recipe Mama had written out for me. It didn't matter how Pig Lickin' good or easy that cake was, I knew I'd never make one again.

* * *

Pig Lickin' Good *was published in* Parnell Hall Presents Malice Domestic: Mystery Most Edible *in 2019. The story, which combines sin and redemption, was a 2020 Derringer finalist.*

Who Dat? Dat the Indian Chief!

Mardi Gras often appears to be a time of decadent sinful celebration, but there are historical traditions behind the various Krewes, parades, and pageants. Sometimes, history and the present collide when it comes to sin, thanksgiving, and redemption.

Charlie Bones waited patiently. Not his usual style, but today was different. Today, he was an Indian Chief. An Indian Chief clad in a regal suit covered with hand-sewn sequins and feathers. He didn't know if he looked foolish or grand under the hundred plus pound weight of his costume, but he knew he was hot.

Standing in the doorway of what had been Al's Liquor Emporium, he decided that taking the chance of being recognized was better than sweating to death. With most of the businesses in New Orleans East destroyed by Katrina, he doubted anyone would pass him in the next few minutes.

He pulled his plumed headdress from his head revealing his full red 'fro. There was no hiding the contrast between his coal-colored skin and flaming hair. The combination had earned him plenty of nicknames at St. Aug before he'd learned to use his fists to demand respect. Now nobody dared call him Redtop, Bonehead, or any of those long-ago schoolboy names to his face.

Charlie knew he needed to get his headdress back on, but it felt good without his masked head covering. He gently wiped the sweat from his brow with one of his feather-covered sleeves before stepping from the doorway to peer down the street. A block ahead of him, he could see the top of the gang's flag. From the erect position of the huge staff decorated with feathers and his group's symbol, he could tell that Spyboy, two blocks ahead of Flagboy, had yet to relay the sighting of another gang.

Try as he might to be politically correct, he had trouble referring to the other four street groups as Krewes. The more typical New Orleans Mardi Gras parades had been lily white, named after Roman or Greek Gods, and used a royalty structure that included kings, queens and pages. Slavery and racism had kept his people from being part of those Mardi Gras Krewes, so they created their own. They paid their respect to the native New Orleans Indians who helped them escape the tyranny of slavery by making up Indian tribe Krewe names that incorporated their street or ward gang names.

Their parades had no set routes. Until recently, they had been a time to settle scores because the New Orleans police were too busy with traditional Mardi Gras activities to interfere. Today's more civilized tribal Krewes used dance and ritual chants to celebrate the distinctive style and art of their respective costumes. Making sure he tucked the knife between his waist feathers so it could be easily retrieved, he feared history might be repeated.

The waiting was getting to him. He felt like he was on a stakeout except this time Charlie was unsure of where his quarry was. A quick movement of Flagboy's staff caught his eye. He watched the circles and angles Flagboy made in the air telling him that Spyboy had spotted the tribe Charlie had instructed him to locate.

Charlie glanced down at his costume. The sequins he had sewn on his vest sparkled in the sun, but there was no question that the jeweled eye of the eagle sitting over his heart was what brought his costume to life. His fingers lingered on it for just a moment before he put his headdress on and grabbed the thick stick he had leaned against the wall of the doorway.

Jumping into the center of the road, he let out three loud whoops and then deliberately raised his rod and banged it sharply on the asphalt in front of the Emporium. He walked about five feet forward and wailed in a birdlike falsetto. Ahead of him, Flagboy mimicked his bird sound and struck the ground hard with his staff. The two of them ran through the same scenario three more times.

From his vantage point, Charlie saw the few uncostumed second liners, who had been singing or playing their tambourines for any onlookers standing between Flagboy and him, stop their entertaining to listen to their exchange. As Charlie and the second liners walked forward, following the angle of Flagboy's now moving staff, the liners whispered his staccato refrain.

Charlie heard the other Krewe before he saw it. He smiled at the sounds of laughter and cries only children can make. Tradition dictated that children didn't march in the Indian Parades because of the violence associated with them, but Father Tom had laid the mothers' fears of their children wanting to join the Indians to rest. His tribe ranged from altar boys to youthful scoundrels, and they followed him as if he were the Pied Piper.

Most of his congregants and students thought of him in that way until Katrina, but the hurricane changed the course of Father Tom's youth ministry. Flood damage to the building's structure, the number of evacuated parishioners who never returned, and the loss of businesses in the area made his church one that the diocese deemed unsalvageable. Like many others, it became part of a consolidated parish. Father Tom still was searching for his position in the new order, but as Charlie had hoped, he probably hadn't lost his place leading his juvenile Krewe.

As the two tribes neared the same point, the old and young of the Krewes mingled together dancing and singing in the street, but they parted to give the two Chiefs room to approach each other. Once the distance between them narrowed to a few yards, the second liners closed in around them.

The two chiefs circled each other, carefully keeping the distance of their huge sticks between them. For a moment, Charlie stared at the opposing Chief's costume of green and gold feathers. He tried to find an unmasked area to determine if the Chief was truly Father Tom, but there was no exposed area of skin.

The edges of a full-faced satin mask that pointed out like a beak were tucked under the ridge of his headdress. Soft tufted feathers sweeping out behind him further accentuated the image of a bird taking flight. Different patches of sequins and feathers incorporated into his costume portrayed stories important to the Chief or his people. They included an image of an eagle similar to the one that adorned Charlie's chest, but its sequined eye lacked the radiance of Charlie's jewel.

As the two faced off, Charlie yelled as loudly as he could. "Humba!"

The other Chief didn't respond to Charlie's demand that he bow and pay him respect. Instead, he stepped into Charlie's private space and began to sway and chant. With each beat of his foot, the volume of his voice rose until he was screaming. "Me no humba. YOU humba."

The two moved toward each other playing out the motions of their war dance. When they were close enough so that they could not be overheard, Charlie said: "Looking good, baby. Looking good!"

His nemesis nodded his head in acknowledgement of the compliment, but didn't return it. "Jewels, Charlie? You gone uptown on me man?"

"Maybe," Charlie said. He'd forgotten only uptown Indians used jewels to finish off their costumes. He figured in the end Father Tom wouldn't hold it against him.

The second Chief stretched his head back and raised his stick acknowledging the sky and sun. He whooped and hollered, ignoring Charlie. In that moment, Charlie whacked his stick against the man's head and neck. Surprised, he whipped his neck back down so quickly that his mask slipped free from his headdress allowing Charlie to catch a glimpse of his alabaster skin.

"What's with you?"

"Just making sure it was you," Charlie said.

"As if you didn't know?"

Charlie extended his hand with the stick toward his albino friend, but Father Tom backed away. "After all these years, you didn't know it was me? What's got into you Charlie? Losing your police detective skills?"

Charlie didn't move as Father Tom made a show of examining his costume from afar. He let Father Tom set the pace for their dance, much as he had let him lead when their differences had brought them together as kids. Back then, who would have thought the two school misfits would grow up to tend the community's soul? Father Tom finally stopped in front of Detective Charlie Bones and bammed his stick two times.

"Humba."

For the crowd's benefit, Charlie shook his head and put his hand over his eagle's eye while loudly proclaiming "No humba." He moved closer to Father Tom and let his stickless hand slide to his waist. "Forgive me father, for I have sinned," he whispered, pulling his knife from its sheath.

He raised the knife between their chests, keeping his focus on his friend's colorless eyes. As Charlie made a swift cut, he felt Father Tom's hand close around his wrist to wrestle the knife from him. "No," he said, as the knife dropped from his fingers, landing next to his now forgotten stick. "You've got it wrong! I'm seeking redemption," Falling to his knees, Charlie pulled at his chest with one hand while instinctively reaching out for his knife with the other before Father Tom could cover it with his foot.

"I humba," he shouted, ducking a blow from Father Tom's stick while shoving his knife back into its hiding place. The stick glanced off his left shoulder. "I humba!"

Father Tom permitted Charlie to pick up his rod and stand upright from his cowered position on the ground, but he held his stick in readiness. The two squared off again, but this time, Charlie bowed to his opposition and with a beat of his retrieved staff and gestures from his arms acknowledged the majesty of Father Tom's costume.

The children surrounding them cheered Charlie's submission while the crowd applauded their Chiefs' throwback portrayal of the historical violence of the Indian parades. Thinking the tribal display was finished, the two spyboys and flagboys resumed their assigned tasks while most of the onlookers and Krewe members fell in together to march and dance in a relaxed parade formation as they searched for more tribes to confront.

With a flourish that appeared to still be part of their dance, Charlie took his hand from his chest and extended it to Father Tom. "Take this. It's for the collection box."

Father Tom shifted his stick to steady it against the ground, but kept his free hand lying at his side.

Charlie turned his hand palm upward so Father Tom could see the diamond lying in his bloodstained palm.

"You're bleeding."

"Must have nicked myself when I cut off the eagle's eye. Guess I shouldn't have been quite so dramatic in the way I transported it to you." He leaned forward to press the stone into Father Tom's hand.

"Where did you get this?"

Charlie ignored the question. "Don't worry about that."

Father Tom stared at the stone. "I don't understand, but I'm pretty sure it isn't something I can accept."

"Tom, look around you." Charlie waved his hand around the desolate street they stood on and then reached out and pulled Father Tom's arm to make him turn to the vacant lot behind him. "Wasn't that where your church was?"

Father Tom nodded, but Charlie didn't stop. He pointed further up the street. "Think about the houses, stores and people who lived and worked in our neighborhood before Katrina. Most all of them are gone. Tell me, what's left for those still here?"

"Hope."

"Hope doesn't buy school uniforms, medical treatment or put food into bellies."

"And crime does?"

"Sometimes, but don't worry," Charlie assured Father Tom. "This isn't one of those times. I wasn't a blue looter. That diamond was part of my planned masking before Katrina ever came along. I wanted to use the jewel on our eagle patch to show people how far we've soared."

"So, why give it to me now?" Father Tom asked, closing his hand around the diamond.

"Because I think your team can do a lot more good with that gem than I can; though," he said, puffing out his chest, "I've got to tell you it was a pleasure strutting from my house with it on my patch this morning."

"I'm missing something here."

"Tom, I've never been a saint, but I took an oath to enforce the law. You of all people know how horrible the looting, trespassing, and disregard for human dignity was with Katrina. Bad enough when it was some punk, but I couldn't stand by without saying something when a few of the blue went bad. Today's parade isn't over for this Indian yet, but just in case, maybe after everything I've seen and done this past year, that diamond can buy me some forgiveness and redemption?"

Father Tom didn't answer. He slipped the diamond into his pocket and banged his stick to let his tribe know he was moving on. He took a few steps away from Charlie, but then turned back and made an elaborate bow toward him. "Who Dat? Dat *the* Indian Chief."

* * *

Who Dat? Dat the Indian Chief! *was included in the* Mardi Gras Murder *anthology published by Mystery & Horror, LLC in February 2014.*

Wabbit's Carat

Greed, diamonds, "pets," and a caper all lead to trouble.

Peter Wabbit wanted a carat. Not just one carat, twenty to be exact. As he walked through the Louvre's Gallerie D'Apollon, he merely glanced at the peached colored Hortensia diamond before going to stand before the case housing the white 140.5 carat Regent diamond. Too many carats. Too ostentatious for his taste.

He stared at the custom-made vitrine in which the Regent was displayed, knowing that when the museum had the cases in the Gallerie D'Apollon redesigned, fiber-optic lighting and more sophisticated alarm systems were installed. It made sense. After all, these cases held the French Crown Jewels.

"It's beautiful, isn't it, Peter?"

Peter jerked his head in the direction of the woman's voice. He hadn't heard the uniformed security guard come up behind him. "I agree, but I think it's a little too big to reset as an engagement ring, Gwen."

Gwen held up her left hand. Together they looked at her long-tapered fingers.

"I guess you'll just have to settle for something more mundane," Peter said.

"And find someone to give it to me."

He felt a warm sensation rise up his neck. Not only had his mother saddled him with the name Peter to go with the last name of Wabbit, but he'd also gotten his tendency to easily blush from her. At least she'd shared her knowledge of how to pick any lock with him. Watching his mother fade away slowly during her last illness, Peter had learned patience. He didn't particularly miss her, but occasionally he acknowledged the skills he'd gained from her—the ones that made him one of the best diamond thieves in the world.

His heists were planned with precision. He didn't just break into jewelry stores and grab whatever was in the showcase. Rather, he specialized in high end diamonds. Consequently, he immersed himself in every detail of a job before executing it.

Two years ago, when Peter decided the five-sided Hortensia diamond was his next target, he managed to get himself hired in the finance department of the museum. Between his skill with languages and the pedigree background he created for his resume, Peter was the perfect choice for his mid-level job. His pasty skin, non-descript features, and hair that matched his thick-rimmed black framed glasses, let him blend in with the other bookkeepers, but his Peter Wabbit name was unforgettable.

People, especially Gwen, were used to seeing him spend his lunch hour in the gallery peering at the jewels and the Louis IV precious stone vases. Periodically, he took one of the museum's guided tours. Peter also knew exactly how many steps and how much time it took to get out of each Louvre exit, walk to either the *Palais Royal—Musée du Louvre Métro* or the *Louvre-Rivoli* stations, and immediately board a train.

The problem was Gwen. She was different. She was the first person he had a desire to share a diamond with. They'd both begun working at the Louvre around the same time. He couldn't remember who spoke first, but Peter imagined it was Gwen. There was something about her independence, her love of life, and her sense of humor that attracted him. When she wasn't on stroll-around duty, Peter hung around her office a bit while he found a way to make a wax copy of her boss's master display case key. Gwen and he had gone out for dinner here and there. She was fun and didn't seem to have any interest in them delving into each other's pasts.

Although he tried to keep her at arm's length, like he did everyone in his life, she snuck into his very being. There were times he felt her green eyes peered into his soul, rather than seeing his Peter Wabbit Louvre persona. Being honest, Peter enjoyed their conversations and flirting almost as much as handling a perfect diamond. Still, he knew he'd never put a ring on her finger. Once the heist was done tomorrow, he'd be gone.

He regretted that while he would get away, lose his glasses, change the color of his hair, and receive a tidy sum when he presented the Hortensia to its private buyer, Gwen would be stuck with the fallout of what he'd done. Not only would their personal involvement raise questions, but there invariably would be criticism about how she neglected her guard duties while helping chase the mice he planned to release.

The mice, those furry rodents with their pointed snouts, small rounded ears, and body-length scaly tails, were going to be the distraction that provided him just enough time to grab the diamond during the public tour. Peter already could feel an adrenaline rush thinking about tomorrow. It saddened him knowing, when the confusion of the moment settled, the scurrying mice would tip Gwen off immediately that he wasn't who she'd thought.

He hadn't meant to introduce her to his fancy mice, but on one occasion, when he'd been running late to meet her for dinner, he'd forgotten to take a little white mouse out of his pocket. When the mouse poked its snout up, Gwen recoiled. Peter had had to take the mouse from his pocket and educate her about it, while he stroked its soft fur.

"A fancy mouse like this is a domesticated form of the house mouse. It really is considered a pocket pet. That's why I forgot about it."

"You have a mouse as a pet?"

"Several. They don't take up much room, are easy to feed, and are fun to watch on their little exercise wheels."

Gwen shuddered. "Somehow I don't think of mice as being my idea of the pet of the week."

"Lots of people disagree with you. There are clubs all over the world who host shows for mice."

"You're pulling my leg."

He smiled and shook his head from side to side. "If you don't believe me, look them up. Some of them in the United States include the FMBA or Fancy Mouse Breeders' Association and the American Fancy Rat and Mouse Association, which is also referred to as AFRMA. In England, mouse fanciers like me can belong to the National Mouse Club."

Gwen hadn't believed him, but the next day, when he visited the gallery during his lunch hour, she'd sidled up to him and admitted, "I went home and read up on the clubs you told me about. You weren't kidding me."

Peter could still picture how he turned toward Gwen and their gazes locked. "I would never do that." He meant it then and he still did, but he hadn't promised that he wouldn't hurt her.

His thoughts continued weighing on him the next day while he prepared for the hoist. As Peter dropped each mouse into the pocket of the specially created vest he wore, it cuddled toward the warmth of his body. He'd spent hours walking around his apartment acclimating the mice to the vest, his body, and movement. Whether they napped or nibbled the cheese he'd placed in the bottom of each lined pocket, the mice were still enough that with a slightly oversized untucked shirt and his sport coat covering the vest, they weren't noticeable either on the metro or when he reached the museum.

Entering through the employees' entrance, despite it being his day off, he greeted the guard on duty. "Hey, John."

"Hello, Mr. Wabbit." John scanned the list on his clipboard. "I don't have you as working today."

"I'm not officially. The boss asked me to look at one report, so rather than waiting for Monday, I thought I'd check it out today and then take the tour. Is that a problem?"

"No, sir. We all know who you are. Go on in."

"Thanks, John."

As Peter passed by him, he hoped John wouldn't lose his job on Monday, especially when the powers that be discovered Peter's empty desk and realized his workspace had been wiped clean of fingerprints. Putting John out of his mind, Peter veered to the main desk and bought a tour ticket. He spent a little time visiting his favorite exhibits, including a moment to engage the device in his pocket to use high-pitched ultra sound waves to disarm the Hortensia diamond's alarm, before returning to the entrance of the Gallerie D'Apollon to meet up with the tour guide.

He looked around, but didn't see Gwen. Strange, she usually worked during this tour. Peter hoped there was nothing wrong. Too bad he wouldn't have an opportunity to find out.

Once the tour began, Peter kept his eye on the guard who was working in Gwen's place while he listened carefully as the tour guide explained about the precious stone vases and the various jewels on display. While the guide extolled the beauty and size of the Regent diamond, Peter held back a few steps from the group. With a flick of his wrist, Peter pulled the string that released the pockets of his vest. Standing still, he felt the falling mice slip to the ground. Free, they scampered in all directions.

It only took a few seconds before a scream or two of "Mouse!" filled the room. As people moved in all directions, Peter went quickly to the case he'd previously disarmed and slipped the key he'd made from the wax image he'd taken of Gwen's boss's key into the lock. He didn't immediately open the case. Instead, Peter took a step away from the case and pointed across the room while he yelled, "Be careful, over there! There's a group of mice!"

It was only when heads turned, women screamed, and people bumped into each other as they tried to avoid the mice that he slipped open the case and removed the Hortensia diamond. Pocketing it, he walked swiftly out of the Louvre and to the metro. Keeping one hand on his pocket, he glanced at his watch. He was right on time for the next train.

Peter willed his heart not to race as he calmly walked down the steps and onto the platform. He peered over his shoulder. Nobody was following him. The train arrived and when the doors opened, he stepped into the filled car. He felt a moment of relief as the doors closed. Against the train's forward lurch, he kept his balance by holding the strap above his head tightly.

Three stops and he'd be safe.

At the first stop, people bumped against him as those leaving jostled those getting on. He automatically shifted his body to protect his pocket. As the doors closed, he looked out at the platform and saw Gwen. She held something up in her hand, blew him a kiss, and then was gone in the crowd. His mind whirled. Could she have?

Peter reached into his pocket. Slowly, he pulled out a rabbit's foot keychain. Attached to it was a paper mouse cut-out. He read the message. "Maybe you'll get lucky next time, Wabbit."

* * *

Wabbit's Carat received a 2020 award in the Bethlehem Writers Roundtable Writing Contest and was published by BWR in January 2021. It was later chosen to be aloud read as a SW Florida Reading Festival Bedtime Story (Bedtime Stories - March 12, 2021 - "Wabbit's Carat" by Debra H. Goldstein - YouTube).

The Girls in Cabin Three

Sunday

Dear Mom and Dad,

First night of camp. They won't let us into the dining room unless I write you a letter. So, here it is. I think they want a letter instead of a postcard to take up more time. Ms. Mott, the camp director, obviously realizes that after six years of being campers, our cabin knows how to dash off two-word postcards.

It's raining and there isn't much to do. The road to the dining room is muddy, but our cabin doesn't leak this year. They moved us to Cabin Three and told us to tell you to put that on our mail. We have new counselors. Their names are Eve and Mary. Eve looks like she could play football. Mary seems nicer.

Five of us are back from last year and we have one new girl in our cabin. I got a top bunk. Carolyn grabbed the one across from me. Yay! Kimi is under her. Like always, she smiles all the time. Her aunt took her to get the neatest cornrows before camp. Unlike Carolyn's wispy hair, Kimi says my thick mop will be perfect for her to do a simple braid.

You remember Iris and Sue, the Jersey twins you met last year? They picked the bunk across the room. The new girl, Denise, got here last. She wanted me to move to the bottom. No way! She's also not thrilled that we've been coming to camp so long that Sweetie Pie, the camp cat, seems to have remembered us. She adopted our cabin as her home this summer. None of us, except Denise who swears she has pet allergies, wants the cat kicked out by the counselors, so the twins are keeping Sweetie Pie on their side of the room. This is long enough to get into dinner.

Love and Kisses,
    Sharon

Tuesday

Mom and Dad,

Still raining. We're spending a lot of time in the cabin or dining room. The counselors say it will be better when it stops raining, and to kick off this week's skits, they got up and sang a stupid song at last night's dinner. All I know is it had a line about some guy named Joe Spivy and poison ivy and another one about Leonard Skinner getting something like potato main poisoning after dinner. After the poison ivy Carolyn and I got into our first year of camp, you better believe that isn't going to happen to us again. I guess we'll have to stop eating the mashed potatoes.
    Sharon

Wednesday

Dear Mom,

I was going to send you and Dad a Polaroid picture of all of us, but—don't get mad and don't tell Dad—I don't know where the new camera he bought me is. I took some pictures and I thought I put it in my cubby, but I can't find it. We're all going to look for it tonight after we work on our skit. The Jersey twins came up with a great idea for a murder plot and I'm writing it. Gotta run—lunch.
    Love,
        S.

PS if I don't find my camera, I'll pay Dad back out of my allowance or set up a lemonade stand.

Thursday

Mom and Dad,

More rain. We can't do anything outside so Ms. Mott sent indoor activity kits to every cabin. I guess she decided we're too old to make braided bracelets because our cabin got a card magic set. Mary only has a few tricks up her sleeve, but Eve is really into it. She even smiled. Boring!

Carolyn, Kimi, and I worked on our murder skit instead. I was going to be the dead body (we took catsup packets from the dining room to make a sponge bag for blood), but we decided it would be funnier to kill a counselor than a camper.

Eve said no way. She can be so-o-oh grumpy. Mary agreed to do it. We were going to make her a pool counselor so all she'd have to wear is her bathing suit and gold whistle, but she said her whistle disappeared. Instead, she's wearing shorts, a T-shirt, and a smock. She'll carry paintbrushes like an arts and crafts counselor. The real arts and crafts counselor promised to help us make props today.

I'm going to be the detective—like Sherlock Holmes (if you open this before daddy gets home, thank him for reading me that book)—and Carolyn is going to be my Watson. Kimi, the twins, and Denise are going to be witnesses and the murderer. I'm not sure which one will be the killer or if I'll make the twins identical killers, but since I'm writing the skit, I'll figure it out by Sunday night.

XOXO

Sharon

Saturday

Mom and Dad,

It stopped raining!!!!!! Some kids went hiking, some swimming, but not us. Mom and Dad, so many things went wrong. First, we were late getting out of the cabin for activities today because instead of making her bed for Ms. Mott's inspection, Denise had a hissy fit that someone took her favorite ring. I saw her wearing it yesterday. It's a lot like the one you gave me when I was ten. You know, a gold band with a pearl on it.

Denise swore she took it off and left it in the cabin when she went to take a shower and it was gone when she got back. Eve, Mary, and Ms. Mott searched the cabin, but no ring (and we didn't find my camera, either).

When Ms. Mott found out about my camera and Mary's whistle, she was upset with Eve and Mary for not having reported our missing things. She grounded all of us "until one of you admits what you did or tells me who took the missing items."

"That's not fair," I said, speaking for everyone as we stared at Denise. "We're not going to fink on each other."

Ms. Mott ignored me, but Mary saved the day. "Maybe instead of making the girls stay in the cabin, Eve and I can take them to the dining room for lunch and then, rather than swimming or hiking, we can practice our skit for tonight." She gave Ms. Mott the funniest sideway glance. "You know, it's the only place at camp that has a stage. We have to rehearse, so if we're in the dining room, no one can write their parents that on the first day without rain they were kept indoors as a punishment for something someone else did."

Before Ms. Mott answered, Denise sat on her unmade bunk, crossed her arms, and pouted. She's such a baby. "I should be allowed to go swimming. It's my ring that's missing. I'm going to tell my father!"

We all glared at her and Ms. Mott looked at Eve, who simply shrugged. "Not another word. All of you will go to the dining room for lunch and stay there practicing your skit. I'll be in my office if one of you wants to talk to me about the missing items."

Even if we knew who took Denise's stupid ring, none of us are going to tell, so we trooped over to the dining room. Denise kept giving Kimi and me the evil eye, probably because we shortsheeted her bed the other night. After lunch, on top of having to stay in the dining room, Ms. Mott made our cabin do KP duty. We had to clear all the trays and sponge them down before we could practice, as well as refill the condiments on every table. Mom, the food after lunch looked even worse than it did before we ate.

We finally got to practice. I gave everyone the props that the arts and crafts counselor helped us make yesterday. Everything was going fine until the part where Carolyn, knife in hand, pushed Mary (I gave Carolyn a bigger part and made the twins my Watsons). Mary was supposed to fall to the ground, stabbed by the aluminum-foil knife Kimi made. Instead, Mary grabbed her side and half jumped and half fell off the stage.

I thought she was giving an award-winning performance. The twins agreed because they applauded, but instead of jumping up and taking a bow, Mary lay on the floor and groaned. That's when I saw that the silver knife sticking up through her bloody fingers was real.

Denise screamed and we all ran toward Mary. Eve reached her first. "Sharon, get Ms. Mott and the rest of you stand in the middle of the room."

When Ms. Mott and I got back to the dining room, Eve was holding Mary's head in her lap. Ms. Mott ran to the phone on the wall and called 911. Then, she called the camp nurse.

The paramedics and our nurse came quickly. When they started to examine Mary, her hands still streaked with red, Ms. Mott sent us back to our cabin.

It was horrible. Everyone was upset. Kimi was crying and repeating the knife she gave Carolyn was make-believe. Carolyn was trying to calm her down by assuring her the knife she thrust at Mary was fake. The twins were real quiet, but I could tell they were shook, too. And Denise was Denise. She pouted.

Ms. Mott came to our cabin a little later. "Mary is going to be okay. It's what they call a flesh wound. She didn't even have to go to the hospital, but we're going to let her stay in the infirmary tonight."

"But all that blood?" Carolyn said.

"Catsup. Sharon, I understand one of the props you made in arts and crafts was a blood sponge."

"Yes, but I didn't get it right. There were sponges in the arts and crafts cabin, but no Saran Wrap. I got a piece from the dining hall while we were doing KP today to make one for tonight." I pulled the clear plastic wrap I'd taken out of my pocket.

Ms. Mott frowned. "Mary will come back to see you tomorrow when she picks up her possessions to go home."

One of the twins asked, "Why is Mary going home?"

"Her time at camp is over." Ms. Mott turned her gaze toward Eve. "Eve, I'd like to talk to you for a moment."

Ms. Mott took Eve into the portion of the cabin reserved for the counselors. It wasn't like we couldn't hear what was being said. You know how flimsy that partition between our bunks and the counselors' area is. I hushed everyone and we listened.

"Eve, Mary told me she saw the missing items in your duffel bag and confronted you about them. She thinks you used a slight of the hand trick to exchange the fake knife for a real one."

"I don't know what you're talking about."

"Let me see your duffel."

"And if I refuse?"

"We'll have to get the police out here. But, if I search your bag and we find the missing things, we can simply return the items and I'll let you go home, too."

"With everyone thinking I'm a thief?"

"We'll simply say the incident with Mary was traumatizing."

I heard a thump, which I guess was Eve pulling her bag down from the shelf and handing it to Ms. Mott. Everything was quiet for a few minutes. When she spoke, Eve didn't even try to keep her voice down. "I don't know how those things got in there. I didn't put them there and I didn't hurt Mary."

"We'll see about that," Ms. Mott said. "I'll get someone in here to watch the cabin, but then you're going to need to come with me."

I may not like Eve, but I remembered what Daddy and you taught me about standing up for what's right. I stuck my head around the partition and told Ms. Mott that Eve might not be a perfect counselor (I know Mom, if I can't say something nice, I shouldn't say anything at all, but I wanted to tell the whole truth), but she didn't take anything.

"Sharon, this isn't about you. Go back with the other girls."

"No, ma'am." I rushed to keep talking before she could say anything. "You need to check the garbage the paramedics threw out in the dining room. If you hurry, I'm sure you'll find the fake knife."

"What are you talking about?"

"Mary and I were going to tape a catsup-soaked sponge wrapped in

Saran Wrap under her smock for tonight's performance. When Carolyn stabbed her by sliding the fake knife between Mary's arm and her body, Mary would press the Saran Wrap, it would pop open, and the audience would see blood. While we campers were cleaning the tables and refilling the condiments, Mary probably made a makeshift blood sponge with one of the kitchen sponges, Saran Wrap, and catsup."

"That seems a little far-fetched."

"Not really. When Eve and Mary were doing card tricks with us the other day, Mary was good at slipping things up her sleeve. I bet instead of up her sleeve, she put a real knife and a blood sponge under her shirt. When Carolyn stabbed her, Mary distracted us by stumbling and falling. At that moment, she pushed the blood pack, cut herself slightly with the real knife, and palmed the fake knife under her shirt."

Ms. Mott hesitated. I guess she was thinking through the possibility of what I'd said.

"I know I'm right and that Mary did it because she's the only one who could have been taking our things. Except for Denise, the rest of us know everything about each other. I don't know when Mary hid those things in Eve's duffel bag, but you can prove what I'm saying if you follow up now."

I was right. Ms. Mott found the aluminum-foil knife scrunched up in the trash with the paramedics' gloves and the wrapping from the bandage they put on Mary. She confronted Mary with the knife, and she confessed.

We're getting a new counselor for the rest of the summer and Ms. Mott offered me a counselor-in-training position for next year. I hope she assigns me the girls in Cabin Three.

Must run.... The sun is still out.

Love,

Sharon

* * *

The Girls in Cabin Three was published in Black Cat Mystery Magazine, Volume 12, in August 2022. That issue of BCMM was designated as a special cozy edition.

A Political Cornucopia

Politics is never pretty, but sometimes the behind-the-scenes action can be quite tasty.

It was nearing Thanksgiving 1969. America had put a man on the moon in July, Kennedy had been dead six years, Nixon was president, and for most of us, it was the Age of Aquarius. For me, after graduating Alabama and spending months banging on doors in New York, I'd come back home and was covering the political beat for my dad's paper, the Wahoo Times.

At 83, the incumbent mayor had decided not to run again. The two main contenders for his job were Sheriff Tom Eden and City Councilman Bob Foster. Ms. Sadie Mae Jones was also running, but as she had been on every election ballot for the past twenty years, the only ink the paper devoted to her was mentioning her name.

Eden and Foster were different. They hated each other and their followers respectively had names like McCoy and Hatfield. Over the years, each had won his job the old-fashioned way—by kissing babies, eating barbecue and buying votes.

Buying votes in Wahoo County is a simple process. Someone the candidate trusts parks a car about twenty yards from the voting station and pops his trunk. The trunk has a bag filled with singles, fives, tens, twenties, and a stack or two of rubber-banded hundreds in it. People come up to the car and negotiate how much it will take for them to vote for the candidate. Once a deal is struck, there's a handshake and a young guy, like me, walks the voter into the polling place. The agreed amount is handed over once the ballot is marked.

I used to wonder why voters didn't shop between the open trunks, but I've learned that once a going rate is established, there isn't much wiggle room. Besides, it wouldn't be considered honorable. Honor is a big thing in Wahoo.

Honor is why Sheriff Eden called a press conference in early October. He stood on the steps of Wahoo's City Hall with his gun and holster prominently displayed against the expanse of his belly. With the microphone echoing his words, he talked to the gathered crowd. "This mayoral election is important to you, the people of Wahoo. You need to elect the man who can get the job done the way you want." Pausing to let the applause die down, his eye was caught by Ms. Sadie, who was standing at the edge of the crowd twirling the parasol she used to protect her pale skin from the sun. He corrected himself to "person" before continuing. "That's why I'm announcing today that I will not tolerate anyone buying votes on my behalf. I'm running on my record." His hand glided over the top of his gun. "I challenge my opponent to do the same."

Applauding, I did what most of the crowd did. I looked over to see if Bob Foster was going to respond. Sure enough, he already was hoisting himself up the stairs. His immaculate white linen suit highlighted his equally white beard and bushy eyebrows. He paused on the steps only when he stood a head above the six-foot Sheriff. Slowly, he leaned forward toward the microphone. "Unlike some, I've never had to buy a vote in my life. So, not only will I not have anyone buying votes for me, I'll offer $1,000 if anyone catches me tampering with your right to vote. Of course," he said, tipping his fedora to the crowd, "I'd be much obliged if you did cast your vote for me." His supporters roared.

Sheriff Eden, not to be outdone, thrust his hand out as he stepped up even with Councilman Foster. He bent back down to the microphone, clasping Foster's hand as the two locked eyes, and said, "Same for me." Then, letting go of Foster's hand, he turned back to where Ms. Sadie stood and, palm upward, extended his hand toward her. "Sadie, will you join us in this pledge?"

Ms. Sadie didn't miss a beat. Moving carefully, making sure not to hit anyone with her open parasol, she joined the two on the steps. "I don't need a pledge to do what's right, but I'm glad you boys have seen the error of your ways." She ignored the matching glares Eden and Foster gave her. "This is Thanksgiving season and win or lose, we should, like our forefathers, give thanks for our bounty. I think the three of us should host a community Thanksgiving luncheon on election day to thank God for the favor bestowed upon all of us."

She fluttered her hand toward the crowd. Sheriff Eden tried to argue that Thanksgiving wasn't for weeks and we shouldn't tamper with its official date, but Ms. Sadie had them over a barrel. By the time she explained that it wasn't until 1863 that President Lincoln proclaimed Thanksgiving be held on the final Thursday of November, and that federal legislation didn't mandate the fourth Thursday celebration until 1941, everyone's eyes were glazed over. No one had the strength to argue with her when she said Wahoo needed its own day of thanks plus the traditional one.

The next morning, the Wahoo Times ran a picture of the three mayoral candidates hanging a wicker horn of plenty, overflowing with fruit and ears of grain, by the stage in the Baptist Church's social hall. Its caption read, "A New day of Celebration - Turkey Eating Substituted for Buying Votes." My editor father had whittled my story about the agreement to not buy votes, the $1000 pledge, the discussion about what to serve, and the candidates joining together to hang the cornucopia as a sign of the abundance of good in this election to a picture and a caption.

If Dad had run my story, people would have known how the three agreed the luncheon needed to be in the church hall so people could eat and vote in one stop. Sheriff Eden had felt if it was at the church, the ladies auxiliary could be coaxed into making pumpkin pies. Councilman Foster had argued it would be cheaper, especially if the community helped out, if the three of them embraced the first

Thanksgiving's idea of fowl by serving chicken, but Sheriff Eden reminded him "Everyone looks at it as being turkey day, turkey."

Ms. Sadie had pooh poohed their main course ideas, suggesting they embrace the historic tradition of lobster and vegetables. When the men challenged "lobster", she started into another history lesson about how seafood rather than turkey was what the first celebrants had served, but Sheriff Eden interrupted her.

"Sadie, I'm allergic to shellfish," Sheriff Eden said. "Besides, lobster would drive the cost of the election skyhigh."

"How? You can each use the money you would have used to buy votes."

"Not exactly," Sheriff Eden said. He looked over at Bob Foster, who was shaking his head slightly from side to side.

"That money's pretty much tied up," Councilman Foster explained. Ms. Sadie didn't question it further. Instead, she suggested they compromise by each bringing something different for the main dish.

* * *

Election day, the church hall was divided almost down the middle. One side had voting booths while the other had round tables set for lunch. Against the far wall, long tables were already piled with big bowls of salad, squash and sweet potato casseroles, cranberry sauce, individually plated slices of pumpkin pie, and sweet tea, but there still was room to squeeze in the bounty from the courtyard.

In the courtyard, three spits were slow cooking the plumpest turkeys I'd ever seen, under the watchful eye of Sheriff Eden. Word was that a few of the county's finest had donated the birds. I couldn't see into the closed grills Councilman Foster and some of the other council members were tending except when they'd open them for a moment to baste their chickens with barbeque sauce. Ms. Sadie was making trips back and forth from her car using a kitchen tray to bring in her little casserole dishes. A number of times, she was helped by some of the voters, who would carry a tray for her, wave "Hey" as they went in to drop off the tray and vote, and then come back outside to salivate at the smell the grills and spits were giving off.

With kids playing on the jungle gym and swings, folks sipping tea and talking, and everyone eager to help bring in the main dishes, the churchyard, just before lunch, reminded me more of a trip to the circus than election day. But election day it was, and when the food was finally in and set up and most of us had filled our plates, Sheriff Eden motioned Councilman Foster and Ms. Sadie to join him on the social hall's stage. Figuring this might be my story or that at least I could get a picture of the three standing under the ostentatious horn of plenty, I put my plate of turkey on the ledge behind the piano, where I could retrieve it later, and moved forward with my camera and notebook in hand.

"I want to thank you all for voting and for joining us in this Thanksgiving celebration today," Sheriff Eden began, holding up his plate so that everyone could see he had filled it with turkey, chicken, and Ms. Sadie's casserole. "Ms. Sadie, I was the first to think this was a ridiculous idea, but it truly has brought Wahoo together in a time of thankful celebration." He recited a short prayer of thanks. When he finished, Ms. Sadie smiled. She took the plate and held it steady so I could get a picture of the three of them under the cornucopia each holding a fork over the plate, but she didn't move to take the microphone like Bob Foster did.

I don't know what really happened right after that. Sheriff Eden had just swallowed a piece of turkey followed by a generous forkful of Ms. Sadie's casserole and Councilman Foster was saying something about it being a fair and positive election when someone yelled out, "Fair? While you guys were cooking, she was buying votes left and right every time a tray of casseroles was carried in."

Someone jumped the guy who was yelling because even if he was telling the truth, it wasn't an honorable thing to share with this crowd. A table went over and the fight was in full force when Sheriff Eden grabbed his holster and pulled out his gun. I thought he was going to shoot into the crowd but he began flaying it around as his free hand went to his throat and he started gasping for air. He must not have had the safety on because when he hit the floor, the gun went off. I heard a whoosh and then a clank as Commissioner Foster dropped the microphone when the overflowing wicker cornucopia dropped like lead onto his head.

Dad ran my eyewitness story of how an abundance of lobster instead of turkey casserole combined with a Thanksgiving decorated cornucopia killed two men and made Ms. Sadie Mayor of Wahoo. The wire services picked it up and wouldn't you know it, my first published story got nominated for a Pulitzer.

* * *

The writing of A Political Cornucopia was one of my earliest published stories when it appeared as the featured story in the November 2013 Bethlehem Writers Roundtable. It was reprinted by Kings River Life Magazine in November 2014

Violet Eyes

Marriage often brings out the best and worst in people.

Sometimes, marriages get stale. It's worse, Roger thought, when they start that way.

He glanced across the bed at Lacey wondering where he'd gone wrong. Pretty, no make that beautiful, he'd been intrigued by her from the moment someone jostled him at the bar and his drink splashed the back of her blouse. She spun around, violet eyes flashing. "What the…," she said, but he failed to hear the rest.

Instead of asking her to repeat her tirade, he apologized, assured her he would pay to clean her blouse, and waved over a waitress to buy her another drink. Lacey accepted the scotch and water and somehow managed to lead him into a quieter corner of the bar. There, whispering and laughing together, he fell in love.

People talked about falling in love at first sight, but the accountant in him knew that was a myth. Ever pragmatic, Roger understood love required attention and nurtured interaction. It was much like the wrinkle free shirts he wore to the office. Each needed to be removed from the dryer and hung immediately to avoid wrinkles.

That night, he noted her alabaster skin and sculptured neck, but her eyes made him throw his lifetime practice of careful analysis out the window. Highlighted by the bar's strobe light flashes, they fluctuated from lilac to royal blue-purple. Over the next few months, Lacey willingly accepted a new blouse and the other drinks and gifts Roger showered on her. She didn't have the money to reciprocate, but it didn't matter. He was over the moon when she said "Yes" to his proposal.

Lacey was quiet at their wedding and subdued as they toured Paris during their honeymoon. Still, he could tell from the way her eyes lit up that she was taking in all the beautiful sights they were experiencing. The satisfaction of sharing those moments with her justified every dollar the trip cost him.

Back in the states, he became busy with tax season, but their monthly credit card bills let him know she was entertaining herself, too. Tax season can be hard on a marriage, let alone a new one, so he was glad she filled her days even if her shopping, lunches, massages, and other activities were a bit extravagant. Each night, when he finally got home, he crawled into bed and whispered to her back, "Only a few more weeks of this insanity. Then, we'll have all the time in the world together."

Some nights she didn't answer him, but most times she would turn in his direction and use her fingertips to softly trace the outline of his face. "Don't worry about our future," she'd say.

But, he had. Carefully, he prepared each client's return with a little bit extra added onto the amount of taxes owed. He sent them their proposed returns, the release for him to file their returns electronically, and a wire address for their payments. Getting everything accurately submitted on time was a nightmare, especially with the extra steps he created using flash accounting software.

Not only did he have to make sure his clients received the proposed returns that included their overages, but he had to transmit their properly calculated returns to the IRS with matching wired payments from his offshore account. In the end, the net amount in the offshore account he'd given clients as the address to wire their payments into was quite hefty.

Tonight, he'd brought Lacey her after tax season gift—the offshore account's balance and two airline tickets to Rio. Roger expected shock or amazement, but instead her eyes softened with tears as she gazed at the account details he'd pulled up on his phone. Glancing from the screen to him, she muttered. "What have I done? You shouldn't have done this for me."

She threw his phone back to his side of the bed. It missed and fell to the floor with a sharp bang.

While he retrieved it, Lacey sat up. She angled her face away from his and through sobs said, "I was waiting for after tax season to tell you I tried, but we weren't meant to be. You're the sweetest guy, but you don't excite me."

She leaned over and took the phone from his hand. Opening her eyes wide, she gazed into his. "I was so wrong."

"And so was I." He leaned over to kiss her and tightly caressed her neck. When she stopped struggling, he lay her back down on the bed and used his thumbs to close her violet eyes now dulled by dots of red. The question of whom his clients would use as an accountant next year flashed through his mind.

* * *

Violet Eyes was published by OMDB! Combining more than one sinful twist and turn in less than eight hundred words was a fun challenge.

The Rabbi's Wife Stayed Home

When one combines technology and marriage together,
the result may be subliminal sinfulness.

I'm not your typical Rabbi's wife. Oh, I bring chicken soup to the sick and meet with any woman who doesn't feel comfortable talking to my husband, but most of Dick's congregants have never viewed me as a true Rebbitzin. They think I spend too much time in the secular world rather than ministering to their needs. I do.

As a psychologist specializing in marriage and family counseling, my clients come from all walks of life. If I provided the same type of services only to Temple members, the people whispering behind my back might think of me as a perfect Rabbi's wife. Of course, I'd probably go nuts.

The reality is that I enjoy being there for congregants, but I need a life outside of them. Besides, I'm pretty good at what I do. I'm also a good mother, loyal friend, ski fanatic, and klutz. Right now, klutz is at the top of my list.

Yesterday, I was coming down the cement steps outside my office when I missed a step. I guess I was distracted because I was texting Ann, my neighbor and early morning bicycling partner, to let her know I wouldn't be riding next week because I'd be at Dick's annual Breckenridge rabbinical conference. I tried to catch myself and save my phone, but I didn't do a good job at either. It's bad enough being stuck at home for the next few weeks in a boot, but I definitely could do without Dick's comments about "being the poster child for the twelve step plan against texting and walking."

Accidents happen. I'm not giving up texting. In fact, I've already texted our kids to let them know I'll be home alone because their dad still insists on going to his study/ski meeting. I also sent one to Ann to see if she rode this morning. From the pings I'm hearing, I'm starting to get some responses:

Hal (mobile): "Hi mom! Sent you a book. Figured with you not skiing with dad this week, you might like something to read while you're home. Feel better."

Ann Roberts (mobile) "No. "Not quite. I went home last night promising myself I would try to be the dutiful wife, but as we lay in bed—him snoring and me seething, I had the urge to kill him. When I found myself debating whether to stab him with a kitchen knife, beat him with the lamp he insisted I turn off when I still wanted to read, or just wait until morning and put some type of poison in his oatmeal, I knew I should leave."

Whoa! I read Ann's message again. A cry for help or a threat? She and Tommy had a rough patch last year, but from what she's shared on our bike rides, I thought that was behind them. Apparently not. This is serious. Tommy could be in danger. I'm obligated as a therapist to call the police if someone makes a homicidal threat, but how can I report Ann?

Knowing Tommy and some of his selfish demands, he might deserve anything Ann does. Slap my face, I can't think like that. I took an oath to report things like this, but Ann isn't my patient. Arguably, that makes my obligation to call the police moral not legal, but what kind of therapist or Rabbi's wife would I be if I ignored her message?

Before I do anything else, I need to talk, or at least text, Ann. Ever since she got a new smart phone a couple of weeks ago, she reads and answers messages almost as fast as I send them. I think she probably sleeps closer to the phone than she does to Tommy.

Robin Goldblatt (mobile): "Got your message. Call me. I need to talk to you immediately. Remember, I'm always here for you."

No response. I would pace around the house or clean my baseboards waiting for Ann to text or call, but I'm stuck in this chair with my foot propped higher than heart level. It hasn't even been five minutes, but I glance at my phone again. What if she does something before she reads my text? I decide to revert to the old-fashioned way of making contact—calling her landline.

Tommy answers. "Hello."

"Uh, hello Tommy. May I speak to Ann?"

"She's out running errands. You can probably catch her on her cell."

"I'll try that. Tommy, by the way, how are you feeling?"

"Fine thanks."

"Would you like to come down here for breakfast?"

"No thanks. I just had a big breakfast."

My heart pounds as my stomach flip-flops. "Oh, did Ann whip you up some eggs or make oatmeal?" As subtle as I'm trying to be, my voice sounds like I'm screeching.

"Nah, I didn't want to be poisoned. I went to McDonalds."

As much as I'm not fond of fast food, today, I hang up the phone muttering a prayer thanking God for the creation of McDonalds. I text Ann again. Nothing. Sitting in this chair, time seems to have stopped moving. I remember what Tommy said about calling her, so I again pick up my cell. Before I can punch in her number, my cell pings. What a sweet sound!

Ann Roberts (mobile): "What's up? R U OK? Do you need me to bring you something? No problem, I'm out running errands."

She sounds calm. I'm not as I type in my next message: "We need to talk ASAP. If you're feeling a little agitated, I'll be glad to listen. Want to run by for a cup of tea?" I don't put the phone down as I wait for her to respond.

She really is taking way too long.

Ann Roberts (mobile): "OMG, I just scrolled up and saw the long message that's getting you so upset. That stuff about the oatmeal isn't mine. It's Cynthia's."

Robin Goldblatt (mobile): "Cynthia's? Let's talk about this…."

Ann Roberts (mobile): "It's part of one of her short stories. She asked me to read it for her and I read it on my new phone. I must have hit something wrong. You have to believe me. It's from one of Cynthia's crime stories!"

Robin Goldblatt (mobile): "I'm so relieved. I'd love to read her story. She always writes such realistic murder pieces. Why don't you forward it to me or have her send me a copy? It would give me something to do while Dick is away. In the meantime, stop by so we can commiserate about whatever Tommy has been up to and how Dick is going skiing without me?"

Ann Roberts (mobile): "Will do. I'll bring lunch over for you and I'll call Cynthia to send you a copy of her story. BTW, Tommy may drive me crazy sometimes, but I'd never put something in his oatmeal ☺."

Relieved and delighted that my lunch will be taken care of, I put my cellphone down. Maybe Ann wouldn't put something in her husband's oatmeal, but I would.

* * *

The Rabbi's Wife Stayed Home received a 2012 Alabama Writers Conclave Humor award and was featured in Mysterical-E in April 2014. The story was based upon a true technological snafu including me, my technologically challenged friend, and our Rabbi's wife, but any final thoughts expressed by the Rabbi's wife in the story are mine—I think.

The Night They Burned Ms. Dixie's Place

I remember the night they burned Ms. Dixie's place. The newspapers reported it was an incendiary, but the only hot thing that night was Ms. Dixie.

Folks who aren't from around these parts chalk it up to being another story from the Civil Rights era. Not as moving as those four little girls killed in the church that got bombed over on Sixteenth Street or as scary as when they blew out the walls of Reverend Shuttlesworth's house. There weren't any men in hoods slinking around that night, and Bull Connor and those dogs the Yankees saw on TV were all sleeping in their respective beds.

What started everything was her belief that she was entitled to run her business the way she wanted. There aren't too many left in this world who heard her that night.

For me, it was the first time I met Dixie Davis. She gave me a nickel. I was nine years old and always looking for a way to make a penny or a nickel. An as extra job, my mom cleaned rooms at one of Ms. Dixie's places at night. Ms. Dixie insisted, unlike that motel on First Avenue, that beds be changed anytime a room got a new customer. Most nights, my mom left me with my grandmother, but when Nana couldn't watch me, Mom would take me along and tell me to sit quietly in the kitchen until she was done working.

I was lying on the linoleum floor, trying to catch a bit of any summer breeze that might come through the screen door, when Dixie came into the kitchen. From where I lay, I had to crane my neck up to see where a red, yellow, and green bandana that matched her muumuu dress covered a shade of pink hair that I'd never seen on a woman before. She had her back to me a she ran water in the sink and washed her hands. Then, she grabbed a glass from the drainboard and filled it with water from the tap before sitting down at the wooden kitchen table. She took a long sip, put her glass down on the table, glanced at the clock on the wall across from her, and rested her head on her hands.

I didn't think she noticed me cuz I was laying on the floor behind her, so I jumped a mile when she said: "What are you staring at, boy?" When I didn't reply, she turned and fixed her eyes on me. I jumped to my feet, but I still didn't say anything. "Cat got your tongue, boy?"

"No, ma'am. Just don't have nothin' to say."

She laughed. "That's not a bad way to be. Wish more men knew how to keep their mouths shut when they don't have anything to say. Come here, boy."

I did what I was told. Stood there and let her look me up and down. She didn't have to tell me who she was. I knew from the way she carried herself and seemed to own the room and everything in it, including me, that she was Mama's boss, Ms. Dixie. "You Maisie's boy?

"Yes, ma'am," I said, but then I was worried my being there was going to get Mama into trouble. "Nana couldn't watch me tonight. I promised not to get in the way."

"Oh, you won't. I can assure you of that. How old are you, boy?"

"Nine."

She raised her eyebrow. I noticed that even though her makeup was on pretty heavy, I could see wrinkles in her forehead. "Mama says I'm small for my size, but I'm strong and…" I stopped talking, thinking Mama wouldn't want me going on and on with her boss.

"And, what?"

"And, I'm a pretty good reader." I stood up a little straighter and stuck my chest out.

She smiled. Then, she reached across the table for a book I hadn't noticed was there. "Think you can read me a few pages from this book?'

I took the book from her, and for a moment our fingers touched; I felt a shock tingle up my arm. "Static electricity," she said. I nodded and looked down at the book I was holding. It was a Bible.

"Do you have a favorite part?" I asked.

"Read me where the marker is."

I started reading the portion she'd marked, the one that walks about a woman of worth. She stopped me after a few lines and took the Bible back from me. For a minute, she looked real sad and then she laughed again, but this time it sounded forced to me. She slipped a hand into her pocket and brought out a leather change purse that she rummaged in until she found the coin she wanted. "Here's a nickel for your reading."

I pocketed it before she changed her mind. Ms. Dixie laughed again. This time it sounded real. "You keep reading and you'll be able to earn a lot more nickels."

"Did you earn this one reading the Bible?"

"Not quite."

I don't know if I made a face or what, but Ms. Dixie grabbed my shoulder and pulled me square in front of her. My face was so close to hers that I could see little beads of sweat on her forehead. I stood there trying not to flinch from the pressure of her fingers pushing into my skin. Instead, I concentrated on the soft scent of her lilac toilet water. She was about to say something else, but my mother came rushing into the kitchen.

Mama stopped short, just beyond the stove. Her hair was disheveled and she couldn't seem to leave the edge of her apron alone as her eyes jumped from Ms. Dixie's hands to me and back to Ms. Dixie's face. "I'm sorry. I didn't have anyone to leave him with tonight." Mama wiped her hands on her apron. I hadn't noticed before how chapped they were.

Ms. Dixie nodded and released my shoulders. I took a step back, out of her reach. "Did you come in here to check on your boy or do you need me for something."

"To find you," Mama said, ignoring me. "We have a problem in the big room upstairs."

"Can you get a few of the girls together to help send the problem on its way, so you can clean up?"

Mama shook her head. She seemed pale and a little short of breath. I stepped forward to help her sit down at the table with Ms. Dixie, but she waved me away. "It's not something I can take care of. I saw Lily go in, but she turned around and hightailed it downstairs. Figured the room was empty so I was going to slip in and tidy up, but I knocked just in case. Nobody answered so I went in with a stack of clean sheets. There was a gent still resting in the bed. I started to back out real quietly, and then I saw a red stain spreading across the blanket. I made myself look again. He'd been stabbed."

Ms. Dixie stood up and put her arm around my mother. "How do you know he was stabbed?"

"There's a knife still sticking straight out of him."

"What did you do then, Maisie?"

"I dropped my sheets and bit my tongue so I wouldn't scream. I knew I needed to find you."

Ms. Dixie's eyes opened wider. "Don't worry," Mama said. "I closed the door tight to make it seem like someone is using the big room before I started looking for you."

Mama raised her head so their eyes locked. "When I didn't see you upstairs or in the parlor, I thought you might be here. It's Mr. Johnnie, ma'am."

"Mr. Johnnie?" Ms. Dixie repeated, letting go of Mama.

"Yes, ma'am. Mr. Johnnie." I was surprised. Mama didn't have to say anything else. Even I knew who Mr. Johnnie was. A bigwig at one of the banks and a friend of most of the city's politicians, Mr. Johnnie's picture was always in the newspaper.

A few months ago I'd actually seen pictures of Ms. Dixie and Mr. Johnnie on the same page. The article said he was spearheading an effort to clean up our city and he wanted to start with the street Ms. Dixie's house was on. I'd read the article and I didn't know what he had against her place. It always seemed to me that everyone was welcome there, but Mr. Johnnie apparently said, "if necessary, everything on the block should be burned." Ms. Dixie answered with some none too choice remarks that the paper didn't think it should print. I didn't understand the whole article but there was no denying Mr. Johnnie and Ms. Dixie were both boiling mad. Guess they'd made up.

"Mr. Johnnie got here about seven with some of his friends. They all know he took the big room," Mama said.

"So, they'll remember where he was when he doesn't come home."

"If he's hurt, maybe his friends can help him…" I started to say, but Mama held her hand up and gave me that look that shuts me up. I decided to get out of their way by sitting down in the corner of the kitchen with my back to the wall.

"What are you going to do?" Mama asked.

"There isn't much I can do except work on emptying this place and then give Mr. Johnnie what he wanted on this street." Mama nodded. Ms. Dixie pushed her bandana back. When she brought her hand down, she must have noticed some dirt on it because Ms. Dixie went over to the sink and washed her hands again. She patted her hands dry on a towel and then used the same towel to dab at her face.

"Boy," she said to me, "there's some kindling and wood on the back porch out there. I want you to bring it in for me."

"Isn't it too hot for a fire?"

"It's never too hot for a roaring fire. Bring that wood into the kitchen and then you scurry on home. Your mother will be along shortly."

I shrugged and glanced at Mama. She nodded and shooed me with her hand. I hurried to do their bidding and then to get out of there while it still was light. It was the first time my mother was letting me walk home alone and even though it didn't get dark until late, I thought it would be a good idea to move before the sun went down.

Mama didn't come home until a couple of hours after me. By then it was dark, which made it easier for us to stand on our porch and see the sparks and flames coming from the direction of Ms. Dixie's house. We didn't say anything to each other, we simply watched.

A couple of days later, I saw a picture in the newspaper of the burning house and one of Ms. Dixie covered in soot from trying to help put out the fire. The article that ran with the picture said someone had thrown a firebomb through the front window. No one knew why. The police thought it was probably a nut or someone crazed by the summer heat.

The fire department was reported as saying they were called too late. The responders tried to put out the blaze, but couldn't save the house or its contents. There was no mention of Mr. Johnnie except to say that the paper unsuccessfully tried to interview him. In the next few weeks, there were a few news stories about nobody being able to locate Mr. Johnnie, but the story faded away like him.

Mama never worked for Ms. Dixie again. She said her day job now paid well enough to keep food on our table and a roof over our heads. I believed her. Mama and Ms. Dixie are gone and Birmingham is a lot different city, but it's my home. I found my niche that night. I've been working as an arson inspector for the past twenty-five years.

* * *

The Night They Burned Ms. Dixie's Place was published in the May/June 2017 issue of Alfred Hitchcock Mystery Magazine. It was named a finalist for the 2018 Agatha and Anthony awards and can be heard as a podcast at
https://www.podomatic.com/podcasts/ahmm/episodes/2018-06-22T06_54_58-07_00 .

So Beautiful or So What

"You holding out on us, Johnny?" The brawny redhead pointed the branch he'd been using to stir tonight's gumbo at me. "What you got in your pocket?"

Ignoring the men and women vying for a spot close to the garbage can fire, I focused on Red. The fact he had me by almost six inches and forty pounds—not to mention that branch, stripped of its bark and whittled to a sharp point—made me want to show him his suspicions were unfounded. The last thing I needed was trouble...and I didn't figure the tattooed words LOVE and MAMA on the backs of his fingers indicated a secretly sweet nature.

I dug a hand into the pocket of my camouflage jacket, drew out the can of okra, and held it so Red could see it. "I didn't realize it wasn't one of those flip-tops when I stole it, so I kept it when I dumped my corn and peas in the pot."

Red stuck out a beefy paw. "Give it here. Who's got a knife?"

There was silence until the new kid piped up: "I have a Swiss Army knife, Red. It's a doozy."

He grinned widely, freckles spread across his face, and held his knife up for everyone to admire, close enough to the fire that flames reflected from its shiny surface.

I groaned inwardly. Thanks to me, the kid would now be a target, soon as Red returned his prize possession. This was not a screw-up an undercover cop ought to have made.

What made it worse was that the kid's slight frame matched the body type of the three victims who'd been murdered under the bridge and in the nearby park over the past six months.

With elections coming up, the homeless and their encampments were once again in the news. The present mayor, the Queens borough president, and their respective challengers were all campaigning on platforms highlighting cleaning up the public areas that had been staked out by the homeless.

The difference between the candidates was in their management of the press after each of the murders. The incumbents dodged the headlines and touted their past accomplishments and future plans, while their opponents—noting that all three victims had been drug users—railed about crime in the streets and the incumbents' failures. The truth lay somewhere between those two positions.

After the second murder, with the uniforms and detectives stymied in their investigation, Paul Landis had been sent in undercover as "Pete Simon." After reconnecting with a former confidential informant, Paul reported making some headway, but the Powers That Be (and Those That Were Hoping to Be), playing on the transient nature of the homeless, thought it best after another month without an arrest to send in someone from a different station. The unspoken explanation was that Landis was what was called by some a SLAP, or "Stupid Lazy-Ass Policeman."

I'd just finished two years undercover on another case, and I was assigned to back up the SLAP. Paul and I had been working the same turf for three days, now, but aside from a nod in passing, we hadn't had any contact. Acting as if I were a bit of a loner, I'd picked a spot on the edge of the encampment to sit and observe its denizens.

Red was obviously the alpha male. Paul had his own group of followers to yuck it up with, including two guys who spent a lot of time shooting hoops in the park, a few who only left their spots under the bridge for the meals offered at nearby shelters, and Larry, who alternated running petty scams with ranting against the police and the establishment. The kid with the Swiss Army knife seemed to be on the fringe of Paul's group. There were also a small number of female members of the loose-knit community—Dishtowel Molly and a couple of others.

There'd been talk around the department about Paul being dirty, but he had a history of making solid arrests. On this case, though, I didn't see any evidence of him doing anything productive, and I seriously doubted any of his hangers-on were the CI he claimed to have.

Meanwhile, now that I'd put the kid in danger over his knife, I'd have to double down on protecting him.

There was something that drew me to the youngster. He just seemed too fresh and naïve to be on the street. Maybe he reminded me of myself at that age. Maybe I thought I could do a good deed and help him turn his life around.

I'd observed Larry using him more than once as the shill in a dice grift. Before the kid continued down that path, I hoped to gain his trust and convince him to go back home— or at least take refuge in a shelter. It's not that I'm some kind of do-gooder, but we *are* supposed to protect and serve.

With a couple of well-placed thrusts, Red opened the can. He handed the knife back to the kid, poured the okra into the pot, and resumed stirring with a theatrical flourish.

"Listen up, yooz guys," he said. "We're going to have a good dinner tonight, and your bellies'll be so full you'll probably sleep like babies, but yooz need to keep your guard up. The cops aren't doing a stinking thing about them three murders."

"Yeah," Larry yelled, waving his hands. "The politicians want us gone, and the pigs'll look the other way until we're all dead."

A frown crossed Red's face, and I figured either he didn't agree with Larry or he wasn't about to be distracted from the point he wanted to make. He waved his stirrer past the bridge. "The first two killings were in the park, but the third one was closer to home, right under our bridge. We got to stay vigilant, yooz hear me?"

Later, with our bellies full and the fire dying, we broke into smaller groups and staked out places to sleep. I deliberately edged near the kid, who was setting up beneath the center of the bridge.

"Supposed to be cold tonight," I said. "It's warmer near the grate on the far side."

"Thanks." He picked up his backpack and followed me to one of the wing walls. I positioned my bedding so I could lean against the bridge's brace, and the kid did the same.

"Want a smoke?" I offered.

"Not that kind." He pulled a joint from his backpack. "This'll relax me more than the stew." He lit up and took a long toke, then offered it to me. As I shrugged it off, Paul materialized, as if drawn by the sweet scent.

"Good timing," the kid said.

Paul smiled. He waved a hand, and Red and Larry joined us. Larry, Paul, and the kid passed the joint around. When it was gone, Paul and Larry got to their feet, but Red stayed on the ground, one of his hands resting on the kid's backpack.

"Be careful where you put your stuff tonight." Red's words were addressed to the kid, but his gaze was locked onto mine. "Most of us've got each other's backs, but you never know."

Looming above us, Paul nodded. "Yeah, we're not all saints. Come on, Larry."

The two of them wandered off. Eventually, Red pushed himself up and sauntered away in the same direction.

Things soon quieted down in the encampment. Lying on my bedroll, I was lulled into that peaceful fullness Red had warned us about. The sky was full of stars, and—even for the homeless—the night was beautiful, so beautiful.

A noise startled me. I propped myself up on an elbow and looked around, finally convincing myself it was nothing to worry about.

So beautiful, I thought, stretching out again, *but so what? There's loads of beauty in the world, but I get stuck dealing with the ugly...*

I woke up a couple of times during the night and checked on the kid. Other than rhythmic snoring somewhere nearby, a few guys mumbling to themselves, and the patter of raindrops on the bridge, nothing much was happening—until just before dawn, when a woman's scream interrupted my dreams.

I jumped up and was second only to Red in reaching the spot where Dishtowel Molly rocked on her knees in front of a pile of rags, a stained towel clutched to her breast. I bent down to see if she was hurt, but she ignored my questions and went on screaming.

Red, I saw, was staring at the rags. When I followed his gaze, I realized that they were wearing shoes. Leaving Molly in the care of the others who'd by then joined us, I bent down to examine the dead man.

Careful not to disturb anything, I circled the body, memorizing as much as I could of the scene. Cell phone pictures would have been useful, but, since I was supposed to be homeless, I'd decided not to carry one. My memory would have to do.

When I saw that the victim was Paul, my poker face slipped for a moment. I glanced up to see if Red had noted my reaction, but he remained expressionless.

I continued my examination. There was no sign of a bullet hole— just a puncture wound in Paul's neck. I was pretty sure the techs would conclude that, like the first three victims, Paul had been stabbed icepick style and left to bleed out.

The detectives investigating the earlier murders had hypothesized that they were drug related robberies gone bad. Seeing Paul's body, I disagreed. The cold-blooded preciseness of his murder suggested an intentional stabbing rather than a reactive killing. I searched for something to confirm that gut feeling.

When I took a closer look at Paul's shoes, I knew I'd found it. Undercover work requires dressing to fit the situation, and Paul's tattered clothes were appropriate for a homeless man—but for some reason he'd opted to wear his own shoes, an unblemished pair of black leather loafers. A robber rolling him for drugs or other valuables would certainly have taken them to wear or sell.

I was also convinced that Paul must have known the person who killed him, since his expression was peaceful, not agitated.

Sirens announced the approach of the police, and Red yelled, "Yooz all need to make yourselves scarce!"

Most of my fellow under-the-bridgers grabbed what they could and scattered. Dishtowel Molly stayed where she was. She'd stopped screaming and sat beside Paul, rocking back and forth, singing in a voice just above a whisper. Her hands still held her towel, which I now saw was stained with blood.

I squatted next to her, close enough to hear that her song was a hymn: "Savior, Pass Me Not."

Red grabbed my arm and jerked me to my feet. "Johnny, we got to get out of here."

I hesitated. "What about her?"

"She'll be okay. If she did this, she'll end up someplace warm. They'll feed her three meals a day and give her a bed with clean sheets. More likely, they'll try to take her to a shelter. She'll refuse to go and end up back here. Come on!"

With a mock salute and an "Aye-aye, sir," I made a beeline for my bedding. It wasn't much—a couple of sheets and a towel that did double duty as a pillow—but it was mine.

As I bent down to collect my goods, the kid stepped in front of me, holding his backpack.

"My knife is missing," he said.

I didn't react—until I saw the tip of a plastic baggie peeking out from between my two sheets.

Either someone was trying to set me up, or my bedding had just happened to be the most convenient place to stash whatever it was that someone didn't want the cops to find. Didn't matter: at that moment, a deluge of blue uniforms blocked any means of escape.

Once the officers separated us as best they could, I had no choice but to huddle under the bridge with the rest of the stragglers, where they wouldn't even let us talk amongst ourselves.

I wound up in the back of a paneled truck with several people—Red, the kid, and Larry—for the journey to the station house for questioning.

Larry again began to rant, and Red tried to calm him down. I backed away from them and found myself next to the kid.

"What am I going to do?" he whispered, clearly terrified. "What if it was *my* knife that killed Paul? Everyone knows I had it. They'll think I did it."

"Did you?"

"No!"

"Then," I said, cupping my hand on his shoulder, "all you have to do is tell the truth."

I knew that my being embedded with this group of homeless men and women would result in my receiving different treatment in the private parts of the station, but that knowledge didn't make the way I was manhandled in and out of the van any easier to take. As we walked into the station, I smelled my own sweat, as pungent as if I'd peed in my pants. No matter how many assurances were made that this was a custodial non-arrest situation, and we were simply being questioned as material witnesses to a homicide, the sugarcoating didn't change the reality that we weren't free to leave.

I kept my face averted from those we passed as we were guided to the elevator bank used to take detained "guests" to the second-floor interrogation and conference rooms.

One flight up, I was the first one out of the elevator. A detective held the automatic doors open for us, and a clerical I'd worked with in the past gave me a big "Hey" as she strolled by. It didn't take a clairvoyant to interpret her realization of her mistake. Her face said it all.

I ignored her and stayed in character, praying Red and company were still far enough behind me to have missed the exchange.

We were brought to separate interrogation rooms for questioning, and the detective assigned to my room—once he'd confirmed my identity—brought me a decent cup of coffee. He debriefed me, then ushered me back to an unsecured area where others waited to be returned to the encampment.

Red sat on one of the benches.

"Can I join you?" I took his grunt as acquiescence. "How'd it go?"

"Probably about the same as it went for you."

"There wasn't much I could tell them," I said. "I was sound asleep. When I woke up enough to realize Dishtowel Molly was really screaming and it wasn't just a bad dream I was having, you and I were the first to react. I stopped to check on Molly, and you checked out the pile of rags and found Pete."

"Well, at least our stories matched."

"They should. That's what happened."

"On the surface, anyway."

"What are you getting at? If you've got something to say, say it." "Getting touchy, Johnny?"

"No more than you." I braced myself in case Red got physical.

He did, but not in any way I would have expected. He threw his head back and laughed.

It took a while before he got himself under control. He leaned closer to me and lowered his voice. "Do you know why Pete died?"

I shook my head.

"Because it was his time."

The hairs on the back of my neck prickled. "And you decided that?"

"Not me, Johnny boy." He pointed toward the ceiling. "Somebody up there called Pete home."

"You believe that?"

He nodded his large head. "We're only given so much time on Earth, and we make of it what we will."

I shrugged. "I don't know if I buy into that."

"I believe existence is a miracle," Red said. "And once I accept that premise, I have to assume that everything happens as planned—or at least within the limits of the choices we can make. Pete made some bad choices."

I dropped my gaze to the floor. Where was this philosophical stuff coming from? And why was Red opening up in the middle of the station house? Was something on his conscience from last night?

I asked him outright, and he laughed again.

"Nah. Never even thought of it that way. Johnny, do you know why I stay on the street?"

"Because it's your home?"

"Not just my *home*." He looked at his hands. "Being out there every day is my *calling*. My mission. Years ago, addiction cost me everything, until a Southern Black gentleman years older than me took me under his wing. He was fired up by the speeches of Martin Luther King, he told me, but it was that picture on the balcony, the one where King's friends are pointing out where the kill shot came from, that led him to realize the power he had. From the moment he saw that picture, he knew he could either live in the past, or he could live the words Dr. King had preached."

Red stared at me. "I was a broken man, but he awakened something in me. I've been clean and sober ever since—and, like him, I took an oath to stay on the street, helping others to find their paths, making sure bellies are full, a bed in a shelter or a treatment program is found, sometimes simply lending a nonjudgmental ear. That's how I interpret redemption."

I didn't know what to say. Either Red truly *had* found redemption, or he was for some reason feeding me the biggest cock-and-bull story I'd ever heard. But why? Had *he* been Paul's CI? That would make sense: he was always out there, observing. But wouldn't ratting people out to a SLAP like Paul be anything *but* redemptive?

My thoughts were interrupted by an announcement that we were being bussed to a nearby shelter for dinner. Nothing was said about what would happen after the meal.

The kid caught up to me while the bus was being loaded. "Thanks," he said. "I took your advice and was honest about going to sleep with my knife but finding it missing when I woke up. Gotta get me another one." He winked at me and strode away from those of us lined up for the bus. Something bothered me about his leaving, but, rather than go after him, I chose to follow the others to dinner.

The meal flew by, with everyone relishing the fried chicken and mashed potatoes, and most of us chattering about Pete's murder and our questioning by the men in blue. After vanilla ice cream and coffee, a good many of us took advantage of the shelter's offer of a shower and a night out of the cold, but some—including Red, Larry, and me—walked back to the bridge.

By the time we got there, I was beat. It would soon be dark, so I headed off to stake out my warm spot by the grate. The kid was already there, with his backpack and some other junk. Before I could get mad, he slid his things to the side, making room.

My bedding was gone. As I tried to figure out how I was going to stay warm, the kid reached into what I'd thought was a pile of trash and handed me a rolled yoga mat. "I always like a little padding," he said, "so I skipped dinner and did some shopping." He patted a second mat. "I figured these would make us both a bit more comfortable tonight."

I didn't have to ask what else he'd picked up while "shopping," because he opened his backpack and pulled out two packaged camp-sheet sets, the store tags still attached. He gave me one. "Sorry, though, no pillows."

I smiled. "I think I can make do without a pillow."

Larry appeared, and he and the kid shared another joint. I stretched out on my new bedding and was asleep almost immediately.

Scuffling and a woman's voice shouting "Not this time!" woke me to the sight of the kid, knife in hand, crouched over me. Dishtowel Molly was straddling his back, riding him like a bucking bronco and pounding him with her tiny fists.

He twisted and turned, trying to throw her off, and finally swatted her, hard, with his free hand.

My body broke her fall, but her weight pinned me in place. As the kid came in for the kill, Red jumped onto him from behind. They crashed to the ground, the kid coming out on top.

As I lifted Molly off me, the kid raised his knife.

"Red," I screamed, "look out!"

Red rolled the kid over with an old-fashioned wrestling move and dropped onto him with his full weight. The kid went limp. Releasing his hold, Red backed away. Blood gushed from where the knife—a new one, bigger than the Swiss Army knife, probably stolen from the same store where he'd lifted the yoga mats and sheets—had penetrated the kid's stomach.

I snatched up a sheet to staunch the flow, but Red grabbed my arm. "Forget it, Johnny. He's gone."

"He was going to do it again," Molly gasped. "He didn't like cops like Paul and you." I stared at her, realizing that she'd used Paul's real name.

"*You* were the CI," I said. She smiled. "The kid was dealing."

Sirens sounded in the distance.

"Marijuana?"

"That and more. Paul was sure the other three victims were customers who got on the kid's wrong side, so he made examples of them. Then Paul tried to muscle in on the action, but the kid had him figured for a cop."

The shoes.

"Paul thought he'd scared the kid into taking him on as a partner, but the kid didn't want a partner and killed him. When I saw him make a move on *you* just now, I couldn't let it happen again."

"You knew *I* was a cop, too?"

"We all did," Red said, "as of this afternoon. You were made getting out of the elevator at the station." He held out his beefy hands, fists clenched. "Your brethren will be here in a minute. I'd prefer to have *you* take me in."

I looked for Molly, but she was gone, blended into the crowd of onlookers.

"I don't see why," I said. "Way I read it, he fell on his own knife. Must have been a drug deal gone bad—I understand the officers found another knife and a stash right around this spot last night."

Red's hands dropped to his sides, and he gazed at me with a respect

I hadn't gotten from him before.

"So," I said, "you making your beautiful gumbo again tomorrow night, or what?"

* * *

Paranoia Blues: Crime Fiction Inspired by the Songs of Paul Simon was published in 2022. Each author was assigned a Paul Simon album and tasked with creating a story using the title of one of the album's songs. I chose "So Beautiful or So What" from the album of the same name— which was Paul Simon's twelfth solo album.

Bucket List Dreams

*Everyone has a bucket list dream. When the dreams
of different people overlap, a whole lot of sinning
just might happen.*

"I want you to get rid of my husband."

Burke Williams rolled the cigar in his left hand, feeling its fine firm texture. No soft spots or lumps. He figured the brunette sitting on the other side of his polished oak desk, much like his late wife, had a lot of the same characteristics as a good cigar. "That's not exactly my line of business. Murder isn't part of the basic job description for a private eye."

She placed a well-manicured hand on his desk. Her polish was subdued. Somewhere between mauve and pink, but not really either. It matched her tailored business suit and showed off the diamond gracing her ring finger. He liked that she didn't soften the masculine line of the suit with a bow or scarf. The ring, which he eyed as being somewhere between four and five carats, accomplished that.

Burke shifted the cigar to his other hand and picked up the clipper lying in the oversized glass ashtray on his desk. On the day Maggie made him her business partner and husband, she threw away his cheap stogies and gave him the cigar clipper and ashtray. He missed her.

"Please, don't," the woman said as Burke used the double blade clipper to snip the end of his cigar. "Cigarette smoke gives me headaches and cigars just do me in."

"Like you want me to do to your husband, Ms....?"

"Mrs. Mrs. Harold Taylor." She sat back in his guest chair. Burke guessed she was waiting to see his reaction to the "Boxed Wine King's" given name, but he kept his face masklike. She had to know there probably wasn't anyone who'd ever watched TV in the state who hadn't seen Taylor's commercials or didn't know how he'd gone from growing up as a foster care kid to becoming the Boxed Wine King.

He had several commercials, all featuring beautiful people with half-filled wine glasses. Burke's favorite was the one where the Boxed Wine King, in a black mariner's cap and white cable-knit sweater, flanked by four or five beauties, sat staring at a picture-perfect seascape. Together, the group extolled the virtues of the sand, sea, and the ease of bringing a box of Taylor wine wherever they were. Thanks to Taylor's humor, the public's hope of possibly meeting someone like one of his models, and the fact that for $10.99 a box of his wine wasn't bad, he was one of the wealthiest men in the state.

Burke lay the clipper and cigar back into the ash tray. He might not have her money or much prospect of any, but he could play the silence game as well as Mrs. Taylor.

Finally, shifting to a more erect position, she spoke. "Perhaps you've heard of my husband?"

"In passing. I haven't seen any new ads for a year or so."

"That's because he's got dementia. His cognitive issues make taping more commercials impossible."

"I'm sorry to hear that. Dementia's a lousy thing." Having once read up on all fifty-six varieties of dementia for a case he had, he knew what Taylor, and for that matter, his wife, were in for. Lousy for Taylor. Rotten for Mrs. Taylor. But not enough for a private dick to cross the line from investigation to murder.

He wasn't sure which was a worse ending—losing your mind or being eaten alive like Maggie was by cancer. It didn't really matter. Unlike the things he should have manned up and done for Maggie, he didn't owe the lady sitting in front of him anything.

This case smelled, and after his last clash with the local authorities, he couldn't afford to get involved in anything that reeked more than a lit cigar. He ran a finger across his still waiting friend, while his focus remained on Mrs. Taylor's face. He wanted to see if her gaze met his.

It didn't. She appeared to be watching his moving finger.

"I don't see how I can help you. Killing people isn't my business."

She reached into the tote bag she'd dropped on the floor and pulled out a folded newspaper. From the picture poking out above her hand, he knew which article had caught her attention even before she shared it with him.

It was the *Journal* interview attorney Robert Dane gave as a veiled kick-off for his campaign for state attorney general. Normally, Burke ignored run-of-the mill political propaganda, but this one had been personal.

The article painted Maggie as a glittering diamond of the legal community who, at a vulnerable time in her life, was taken advantage of by a loved one. If elected, Dane vowed prosecution of Burke for Maggie's death, as well as going after anyone else who harmed the elderly or the ill. While mainly campaign rhetoric, the article sprinkled indirect suggestions about Burke being a gigolo amidst direct quotes about euthanasia and opioid overdoses. It ended by guaranteeing that a vote for Dane would ensure a voice against opioid abuse and mercy killing.

The middle portion of the interview was burnt into Burke's mind as clearly as the picture Dane staged in front of the flophouse Burke had lived in after walking out on Maggie. It was where she was found dead. Pointing behind him, Dane expressing disgust for how a husband and individual who worked within the law could have sunk below the boundaries of both.

Dane conveniently forgot to mention Maggie had come to the flophouse, dragged Burke off the bed, and then made him shower, shave, and promise to give up booze. Or that, after promising to turn over a new leaf, Burke left Maggie resting on his unmade bed while he went to get them some sandwiches. Despicable liar that he was, Burke stopped to buy a box of Taylor wine. The guy at the liquor store and the time on the receipt were what unraveled the case against him.

Burke waved his hand in the direction of the paper. 'I'm sorry if you got the wrong impression. That article misrepresented the circumstances so badly they printed a retraction."

"I must have missed it."

He wasn't surprised. It ran on page twenty-four.

She tapped the paper. "Even so, what is here, tells me you understand my situation."

"Maybe, but like I said before, I'm not about to jeopardize my license by killing someone."

"You won't be jeopardizing anything, and you'll be well-paid." She reached into her tote again, retrieving a white security envelope.

Burke wondered why she'd bothered with a security envelope when she left it unsealed.

As she dropped it on his desk, he saw the few bills poking out were hundreds.

"I don't want you to actually kill him. I want you to help me kill him with kindness."

"Excuse me?"

"You're a private investigator for hire, aren't you?" She didn't wait for him to answer. "I want you to protect my husband while helping him live out his bucket list."

"Now, I'm the one who doesn't understand."

"It's quite simple. I love Harold or at least I loved the Harold I married. Unfortunately, a lot of his thoughts concentrate on pleasurable things he enjoyed in the past and things he wished he'd done. I want you to help me check things off his bucket list before he can't…"

She rested her hand under her chin. The glint of the solitaire gracing most of her ring finger again caught his eye. He wondered how he missed seeing it was a marquise cut when he sized her up earlier. Maybe because he'd been comparing the size of her diamond with the small round one he'd given Maggie.

"Can you tell me there was never a day when your wife was ill that you didn't wonder how you could extricate the two of you from the situation you were in?"

He desperately wanted his cigar. She was getting too close to feelings he fought against remembering. Burke forced himself to meet her gaze.

"Never."

"Then you're a better person than me." She turned her head away from him and brushed under her eye with the forefinger of the hand with the rock on it.

Burke couldn't decide if she wiped a tear away or was simply acting for his benefit. Either way, the moment passed, and she looked at him again. "There are days I need a distraction."

"How about shopping or a movie?"

"Don't be flippant. That's not what I mean."

She gave him a look that made him think she might be reconsidering her presence in his office but picked up where she'd left off. "I can sit outside with Harold, hold his hand, or stroll our garden with him. I can even wipe drool from his chin. Every day when I do these things, with my good-wife smile pasted on my face, each of us dies a bit more. That's why I want to do something special for us now."

Hence, the bucket list, Burke thought. Did he sense some guilt there, too?

"Wouldn't a round of tennis do for you? Surely, the wife of the Boxed Wine King can afford hired help. You could duck out for a few hours each day to work out, play tennis, go to the beauty salon, or get to know the tennis pro?"

"That's not my style. I took a vow of in sickness or in health when I married Harold. I intend to stand by it, but I need to do something with my mind while he loses his."

Burke understood. He'd tried alcohol before moving out. Maybe her idea was a better way—that is, unless she tried to go from make believe to reality.

"How did you come up with this killing kindly idea?"

She smiled. It was engaging. Somehow, she managed to press her lips together, but show a hint of her teeth. Unlike Maggie's, which had had a slight gap between the two front ones, Mrs. Taylor's were perfectly uniform. He figured they were capped.

"I asked him what things were still on his bucket list. He said he wished that before a friend died, they'd visited the places they loved as children. When he told me about how they watched seagulls soar at the beach and grabbed for the Watch Hill Flying Horse Carousel's brass ring, I decided to arrange for Harold to visit those places again."

She stood, her hand on the newspaper. "We both know how easily people jump to the wrong conclusions. I had an MBA when I went to work for Harold's company. Most folks think I married him for the benefits that came with being his trophy wife. None of them credit Harold with having been impressed with my brains and abilities. They discount we married for love."

Burke eyed his cigar again. "Love isn't always everything it's cracked up to be."

"Maybe not, but it was for us. Whether he was rich or not, I'd have married him."

"If you love him so much, why don't you simply take him to these places?"

"Now that I'm running the company, I don't have that kind of time. Besides, call me paranoid, but I want to make sure no one harms Harold during his trip down memory lane."

"So, hire an attendant who drives. It's a lot cheaper and makes more sense than hiring a private detective."

"He has an aide. The problem is his attendant, without a gun and the right reflexes, can't keep him safe. I think someone is trying to harm him."

Burke frowned. He'd heard this broken record before. "Why?"

"About a month ago, Harold and his helper planned to spend the day where Harold filmed his beach commercial. Have you seen that ad?"

"Yes." Mrs. Taylor didn't need to know that he was well acquainted with the white sand and pristine water in the ad. He'd spent many pleasant afternoons on that beach with Maggie.

"Apparently, Harold's aide parked near the beach. When they went to cross the street, a car veered toward them. His attendant heard it and barely pushed them out of its path. It sped away, but Harold's helper was sure it was aiming for them."

"Cars swerve. Pedestrians get hit all the time. Is that it?"

"No. Someone knocked him over in the mall last week."

"Sounds like you should take this information to the police, not me."

"I did, but because I can't prove anything, they simply took my report." She stood and pushed the envelope closer to Burke. "If I wanted to learn the ins and outs of playing tennis or golf, I'd hire a pro. That's exactly what I'm doing now to fulfill Harold's bucket list."

"Not exactly." Burke could imagine a tennis or golf pro embracing her trim figure from behind while showing her how to swing through her shot. He doubted that came with his assignment.

"Maybe not with the same level of contact."

He recoiled, feeling she'd read his mind.

She laughed. "I think five hundred dollars for a retainer, plus your daily rate and expenses up to $5000 for two or three days of work is fair, don't you?"

"More than enough if I take your case, but this doesn't really seem like something up my alley. It feels like a game with me somehow being played as a patsy."

A line creased her forehead. "I assure you that's not the case."

Burke's hand again found its way back to his cigar. This time he picked it up and twirled it between his fingers.

"Why don't you light that up after I leave while you think about my offer? Personally, I feel certain that after a few calming puffs, you'll agree this is a win-win proposition for both of us. My number is on a card in the envelope."

Mrs. Taylor didn't wait for an answer. She headed toward the door.

He picked up the envelope. "Wait a minute. I need to give you a receipt for this."

She looked back over her shoulder. "Don't bother. I trust you. Hopefully, you'll trust me, too."

A grunt was the best he could do as a reply, but when she let the door close behind her, he assumed it satisfied her.

As he waited for his computer to power up, his hands immediately followed her direction to light up. Waiting for the start functions to end, Burke held his cigar above the flame of his torch lighter. He spun the cigar around to get an even burn. Rewarded with an orange glow, he popped it into his mouth and puffed rapidly, expelling smoke until its whiteness let him know the end was well lit. The process might not be as numbing as Taylor's wine, but he knew this habit would have satisfied Maggie as much as it did him.

Savoring the flavor of the cigar, Burke picked up the envelope. He trusted Mrs. Taylor enough not to count it. Dropping her card on his desk, he shoved the escaping bills and envelope into his desk drawer, next to his gun.

Pulling a legal pad on his desk toward him, he picked up a pen and drew a vertical line dividing the page into two columns he labeled "Yes" and "No." Under "Yes," he wrote "$3000–$5000." His "No" side, with "patsy, something rotten in Denmark, pretty gams, shiny diamond, and not fully believable," was longer.

Burke studied the two lists. He circled "Yes." Money and jobs had been scarce since Maggie's death and Dane's accusations. Maybe this job would turn things around for him.

After taking a long drag off his cigar, he decided the beach held too many memories for him, so he'd take Harold to the carousel first. Tapping his cigar out, he retrieved the card with her phone number.

She answered after the first ring.

"Mrs. Taylor, I've decided to take your case. I figure we'll start with the merry-go—"

She cut him off. "Good. Harold is up early, but usually naps in the late afternoon, so why don't we say I'll have him ready for you tomorrow at eight."

"I can make that work."

She hung up.

At exactly eight the next day, Burke stood outside the Taylor home. For comfort, he patted the cigars he'd put in his breast pocket and then rang the doorbell. Standing in front of the oak-paneled door, he imagined, from the house's size and the neighborhood, it had at least six bedrooms and eight baths. He fully expected a maid, but the door was opened by Mrs. Taylor.

Barefoot, she wore a ruffled white shirt and black denim pants. Her diamond earrings and pendant were each half the size of her ring. He assumed the stones decorating her jeans were rhinestones rather than diamonds, but then again.

"Come in." She stepped back from the door, so Burke could enter the two-story entry.

There was no question that his entire apartment could fit into it. A giant-colored glass chandelier overhead caught his eye. He'd seen things like it before, but only in magazines or museums. He pointed to it. "That's quite a piece."

"On our honeymoon, Harold and I stumbled into a small shop in Murano. We fell in love with the glassblower's work. When we got home, we couldn't forget it, so Harold commissioned him to make one for us."

"And you shipped it here?"

"Yes. Once blown and put together, the fixture had to be disassembled, shipped, and reconstructed under the watchful eye of its creator."

"Sounds like an expensive project."

"Harold always says, 'What's money for if you don't spend it joyously?'"

Burke glanced at the chandelier and the art strategically hung in the entranceway. "Has it brought you happiness?"

She shrugged as she led him into a library that could have come out of a Dickens novel.

Her husband sat in a leather wingback chair. There was no attendant in sight.

Burke immediately recognized Taylor from his TV ads and, he realized, from some charity function Maggie dragged him to.

Taylor smiled at Burke. "Have we met?"

"No."

Mrs. Taylor laid her hand on her husband's shoulder. "Harold, this is Burke Williams. He's here to help you check off some of the items on your bucket list. Today, the two of you are going to visit the Flying Horse Carousel. You're going to have it all to yourself for at least an hour or two until it opens."

She bent and pecked Harold's head.

He glanced up at her and smiled. Harold turned to Burke. "Hello."

In the car, after glancing over to make sure Taylor's seat belt was fastened, Burke pulled away from the house. It was a short drive to Watch Hill. Not saying much to each other, they walked down still empty Bay Street toward the wood-framed pavilion that housed the carousel. Nearing the structure, Burke could see it was ten-sided with a hipped roof.

Hearing an intake of breath next to him, Burke turned to make sure his charge was okay. Taylor was staring at the carousel. Burke followed the direction of Taylor's gaze. The merry-go-round had about twenty gaily painted wood horses of two different sizes. Chains attached to the rump and an iron bar at the pommel of each horse suspended them from sweeps radiating out from below the canopy at the center of the carousel. "Do you want to wait around and take a ride?"

Taylor laughed and nodded toward a bench facing the merry-go-round. "I think we'd be better sitting over there and looking at it. You look a bit over the one-hundred-pound weight limit."

"I can stand next to you if you want to ride."

"Don't think that will work either. There's no floor to stand on. That's what, for the past hundred and twenty-five years or so, helped make this a unique attraction."

Burke glanced at the merry-go-round again. For someone who observed for a living, he'd missed that one. Maybe he'd been in the office too long.

Taylor continued staring at the carousel.

Burke didn't interrupt whatever Taylor was thinking about.

When Taylor finally spoke, his gaze didn't shift. "I'm sure you've heard how I bounced around between different foster homes. Some were good, some not. Making friends was difficult because I moved so much. When I was nine, I spent almost a year near here before I was shuttled off in the middle of the night. I always regretted not saying good-bye to the one friend I'd made. The moments she and I rode this carousel made the rest of my life bearable."

Taylor sighed, lost in his thoughts again.

"The carousel is built so that as it spins, the horses move away from the center making you feel like you're flying. From an outside horse, you have a chance to win another ride by grabbing a brass ring as you fly by it. I never had much luck, but my friend was successful almost every time. Because I had no money and she did, she always insisted I take the free ride."

"Sounds like a special friend." Burke assumed this was who Mrs. Taylor had mentioned.

"She was. A one in a million saint." Taylor reached into his pocket and pulled out a brass ring. He handed it to Burke.

Turning it over in his hand, Burke observed how scratched the brass was. "I never got to use that ring for a ride, but no matter where I moved, I kept it. I hoped if I found her again, I could propose with it."

"But you never found her?"

"I did." Taylor turned his head and met Burke's gaze. "She already was married."

"That must have been a gut kick."

"I could accept that. After all, I'd already been married once."

"So?"

"She married a bum." Taylor spoke faster. "I begged her to leave him, but she refused. I swore he'd hurt her. She disagreed. She believed he was redeemable and, more importantly, she loved him. When Maggie walked away, I promised that if you hurt her, you'd pay."

Burke recoiled. "My Maggie?"

Taylor nodded and grinned. "I may not remember where I put my keys or what I had for lunch but getting even for her is at the very top of my bucket list." He lunged at Burke, who pushed him away.

When Taylor didn't come after him again, Burke stood.

"I wouldn't do that. Sit down," Mrs. Taylor said.

Burke whipped his head toward her voice and stared at the gun in her gloved hand.

During his scuffle with Taylor, he hadn't heard her come up behind them. Had she been waiting on the far side of the carousel until this moment?

"Put your gun on the ground and kick it toward me. And don't get funny. I'm a fairly good shot."

He sat and complied.

Keeping her gun aimed at him, she squatted and picked up his gun.

"Why?" Burke asked.

"I told you I'd reached the point I needed to do something for both of us. Once I shoot you, the top item on Harold's bucket list will be checked off. His fingerprints will be on the gun, but with his dementia and a good lawyer, Harold will be institutionalized for the rest of his life. That will check off the only thing on my bucket list."

"But there was nothing between them?"

"Not physically, but Harold never gave up hoping. Do you know what it's like having three people in a marriage? Harold loved me, but he never stopped loving your wife more."

Burke felt the bullet slide by his cigars into his chest. As he slumped against the back of the bench, a red stain spreading across his chest, he saw the sparkle of Mrs. Taylor's diamond as she pressed her husband's hand around the gun's grip. His last thought was whether the new Boxed Wine Queen would raise a glass in his memory.

* * *

The challenge for Murder by the Glass: Cocktail Mysteries (Untreed Reads 2021) was to include wine in the story. For fun, I decided to mix a touch of noir with the concepts of sin, forgiveness, redemption to see which one would come out on top.

Harvey and the Redhead

When a detective, storm, and family squabble collide,
redemption becomes a pentimento moment.

"Harvey. Not exactly the most popular name in Houston right now." The redhead pointed to the Noir Night name tag pasted on my brown blazer's lapel.

I gave her a second look. She was pretty. Not a cute pretty, but the genuine siren type beauty that would knock most guys' socks off. Not mine, though. I've sworn off blondes and redheads. "Maybe not. But, the name suits me."

She took the barstool next to me and crossed her legs in my direction. I didn't even try to avert my eyes from her perfectly formed gams. Why bother? My gaze didn't faze her one iota. Either she was used to men staring and drooling or she was deliberately provoking me. When she inched her skirt up, exposing more thigh, I decided it was both.

I bit.

"Rather than a few hours of escaping Houston flood stuff by taking part in Open Mic like me, I get the feeling I'm your target tonight. Why don't I buy you a drink and you tell me why?"

The laugh that erupted from her cherry-red lips, when I signaled for the waiter, was deep and throaty. What you'd expect from a Dashiell Hammett or Raymond Chandler character or a dame like this one. I pulled a pack from my pocket and offered her one. She took it. It dangled from her lips until I lit it. Then, she let it lightly rest on two fingers as she removed it from her mouth and blew smoke rings over her shoulder.

In this era of non-smokers, I doubted that ever deterred her. I guessed she was trying to conjure up my memories of Bogie playing off Bacall or Bergman, but her style might simply have been influenced by what we'd heard over the microphone during the last hour. Or, maybe she and I belonged back in the golden era of hard-boiled detective stories and noir. I like to think the stories I grew up reading made me become a private eye. Then again, maybe not.

No matter. Considering this was the first night in four I wasn't lying awake in a shelter fretting about how much I lost when my Meyerland place flooded, I had no intention of being in working mode.

"Scotch neat for me," I told the waiter. "And the lady will have…"

"A vodka martini with two olives."

I looked at her more closely. Unlike me, her face was unlined and, rather than needing a tint or Grecian Formula, the red was natural. No question, she wanted something from me or she'd be doing something better with her time. I doubted she even knew the names of the writers or any of the characters whose names were being tossed around during Open Mic.

The waiter brought our drinks. Without a toast to each other, I drank about half of mine and tapped my glass for a refill. Might as well be fortified for the evening. In good time, I'd find out how she knew to find me here.

I waited. There's a lot of waiting in my business. Sometimes, it's a stakeout to get pictures of a philandering husband or a kid as he finishes servicing an older guy's young wife or mistress. Most of the time, it's a matter of going through dusty records, doing internet searches, or using old-fashioned legwork to find someone or something. Occasionally, I'll pretend to be a meter man or delivery guy to get close enough to talk to a neighbor or take a closer peek through a window or door. This gal didn't give me the feeling any of these things would be what she wanted.

"You know my name, so why don't you tell me who you are. Or, should I call you Double Olive?"

She laughed again while the waiter replaced my empty glass.

"Olive actually is right. Olive Twist." When I raised an eyebrow, she added, "Really."

"Sure." I don't like to be played. Next thing she'd tell me she was a cousin to those Hogg sisters or part of that Tree family who named its kids Christmas, Pine, and on down the line.

She sipped her drink. "You've heard of Twist Realty and Development?"

I sat up straighter and mentally clocked in. There might be a good fee in whatever this was. "Yeah."

"Last year, you discreetly helped my Uncle Jack resolve a problem. He thought you might be able to do the same for me."

"It depends. I don't take just any case." I twirled my glass around thinking I should have ordered it on the rocks so I could have made the ice clink a bit. Although I wasn't looking for work tonight, Harvey'd made it necessary for me to find a gig soon.

Things were slow before Harvey and who knew what the storm's aftermath was going to be for dicks like me. The three shirts, blazer, and two pairs of slacks I'd salvaged from my old place didn't take up much space in my newly provided FEMA closet. They were going to need some company, especially if anything went to the cleaners. Hopefully, whatever Olive wanted wouldn't take me to the cleaners.

"I understand. But Uncle Jack, he's my dad's business partner but not really a relative, thought this might interest you—especially since you live in Meyerland."

"That's a bit debatable this week, but I'm listening."

"I need a painting retrieved."

I held up my hands framing a small picture. She shook her head and spread hers wide. Without seeing it, I had the feeling her painting would dwarf any wall in my old house, if it still had walls.

"That seems a pretty big painting to misplace. Was it stolen during the storm?"

"No, years ago, but it turned up the day before Harvey."

"If you know where it is, what do you need me for?"

"To get my painting back without involving me or any of my family."

I sipped my drink and bent closer to her, my eyes never leaving her face. This time, it was she who waited me out. I was impressed. Silence usually works in my favor, but I'm the one who ended up speaking first. "It sounds like this is something better suited for the police than a private detective."

She asked for another cigarette. I gave it to her and flicked my Bic to light it. Olive inhaled before slowly blowing the smoke back at me. "That would be complicated. I never reported it missing."

"It's hot? Something bought on the black market?"

"Nothing like that. Uncle Jack painted the picture. When my grandfather and he were young, they got into art as a cultural thing. They studied and began buying what's now the Twist-Griswald collection. Uncle Jack also tried his hand at painting. The missing painting hung in his study, but because I liked it, he gave it to me when I was fourteen. It has sentimental value but no economic worth."

Consciously, I relaxed the furrow of my brow, but couldn't fully erase my frown. "I think I'm missing something here. Your Uncle Jack isn't a famous artist whose paintings carry great price tags. Nor is he someone infamous enough for his works to command top dollar, like those of Eisenhower, Churchill, or that ex-president who paints in Dallas. So, why avoid the police?"

"Two reasons. First, because my name is Twist." She shoved a copy of the previous day's *Houston Chronicle* at me.

I glanced at its front page while listening to her. The two-line headline read: "Artist Daniel Jones Rescues Ten/Dies Trying to Save His Own Paintings." The picture showed standing water licking the bottom of a couch. From a dark slash on the wall behind the couch, I could tell the water had significantly receded from its high point. A painting of one of our local parks was centered over the couch, just above the flood line.

I skimmed the story. Apparently, Jones, a local artist whose name I even recognized, used a rubber dinghy and electrical cords to bring people from his house and two sets of neighbors to safety from the hurricane's swirling waters. When there was a lull in the storm, he returned home to retrieve his favorite pieces of artwork, but something went wrong. Responders checking for stranded people spotted him lying face down in the muck in front of his house. It was unknown if a tree limb or piece of falling debris hit him. He was pronounced dead at the scene of the accident.

"And two?"

"And two, because the article doesn't mention if the police are investigating this as a suspicious death. If Uncle Jack or I become involved, the police will stop looking for suspects."

I pushed the paper back to her, without asking if one of them did it. My finger rested on the painting hanging over the couch. "Is this a Jones original or the painting you've been talking about?"

"It's the one I told you about. I want you to get it back and find out who killed Daniel."

"Whoa. One thing at a time. You said your Uncle Jack painted it, but if you had it, how did it end up hanging in the living room of a prominent artist?"

She rubbed the stub of her cigarette out in my empty drink glass and glanced out the window. "I don't know why Daniel hung that painting there instead of one of his own. Perhaps it reminded him of the best of times or what it was like before he made it as an artist."

"I still don't see this as a job needing a private eye." I let my words play in her mind. This time the moment of silence worked in my favor.

Her gaze met mine. I searched her face for some sign of warmth, but the now rigid line of her jaw matched the ice blue of her eyes. "Getting the painting back might not need a private eye, but finding out who killed Daniel does. You see, if the police are worth two cents, they're going to think I did."

She paused. I didn't give her the satisfaction of showing my reaction, but my brain churned, wondering what exactly she'd left out of her story. "Why?"

"Because I'm the black sheep who ran away and married a struggling artist named Jones. It took a lot of heartache and physical pain before I realized my family was right about him." She laughed again, but not in the genuine manner of before. "I chased him and his bimbo down our driveway using the bumper of my car to help him increase his speed. Uncle Jack handled the details of smoothing things over, but I'm sure the bimbo, who was one of the people Daniel saved, remembers me yelling, 'I'm going to kill you! If it's the last thing I do, I'm going to see you dead.'"

"But, no pun intended, that seems like it would be water over the dam now."

"It would be except Daniel came to see me last week."

I leaned back on my stool, holding my hands in the meditative position where the fingertips from each hand touch each other as if in prayer. "How did he know where you were?"

"Everyone knows I'm always at work. Since my grandfather died and my father has been involved in the business less, if anyone needs anything at Twist, it's call Olive." She ran a manicured finger, tipped in a color that matched her lips and hair, around the rim of my empty glass. "After my divorce, I joined the family business and became a model employee."

"What did Daniel want?"

"For me to anonymously underwrite a showing of his work, for old times' sake."

"Did you agree?"

"Hell, no. I told him I wouldn't be blackmailed by a two-timing wimp. I pointed to the door and suggested he be careful lest it hit him on the way out."

"And?"

"He made some nasty cracks, but left. Once I knew he was gone, I locked my office door, put my head on my desk, and had a good cry."

I couldn't imagine her face splotchy. "Crying about him or what he had on you?"

"You're perceptive," Olive said. "At the time, I could have made a scene about his behavior during our marriage, but he had me over a barrel."

She paused to wave the waiter over for another round. Figuring I'd better get something in my stomach, I grabbed a handful of shelled peanuts from the community bowl sitting on the bar. I've always been good at holding my liquor, but if I wasn't careful, Olive was going to put me to shame.

"When we married, I thought Daniel was family, so I didn't keep any secrets from him. Unfortunately, or should I say unwisely, I told him a few things that would have been better left unsaid."

"But you're going to tell me?"

"Uncle Jack said it would be the only way to gain your interest."

I nodded. Apparently, Jack sized me up quickly and accurately during our past dealing. Olive had my complete attention, and maybe my cooperation.

"My family tries to be honest in all of our business dealings, but my grandfather made a few deals he wasn't very proud of."

"Crooked?" Interesting. Most stories I remembered about the Twist grandfather were about him building his business and giving back to the city through anonymous donations. There was scuttlebutt about an insurance settlement the old man received after some of his art was stolen, but I couldn't recall anything that painted him or the Twist family in a bad light.

"Far from it. How much do you know about the Meyerland area?"

"Not much. When I moved to Houston last year, I was told it was a desirable location because of lots of ethnic diversity, good schools, and nice green areas."

"Did your realtor mention flooding from the Brays Bayou?"

"In passing. Her spiel stressed Meyerland's community atmosphere and parks."

During the past few days, while lying on my cot, I'd pondered suing my realtor for her minimal disclosure that Brays Bayou, which now has flooded three times in three years, is a swampy waterway coursing through the city carrying runoff to the Gulf of Mexico. When I mentioned it to the FEMA adjuster, he scoffed at my idea. Seems I didn't read the fine print of my house closing documents. I'd splashed my John Hancock across papers specifically divulging I was buying in a designated flood zone that previously flooded. I even initialed both the recommendation and my declination of flood insurance. That put the monkey of not taking out insurance squarely on my back.

Olive nodded. "Your realtor was right about about Meyerland being diverse and a good place to live. It's what persuaded Daniel and me to buy what I thought was going to be our forever home there."

She snorted like a hog. I did a doubletake. It didn't fit my ladylike image of her. "Because Meyerland has a reputation as a Jewish hub, but also as being tolerant of all immigrants and faiths, I thought it would be diverse enough for us to create a home that embraced art, friends and our love. Turned out, like the Brays Bayou, Daniel tended to wander."

She was wandering now, so I prodded her back to telling me her grandfather's story.

"Sorry," Olive said. "As I'm sure you've heard on the news this week, Houston doesn't have a zoning code, so builders neglected to incorporate flood protection provisions. Over the years, Meyerland flooded, but not widescale enough to spur a demand and response to the bayou overflowing until 2001."

"2001? Did I miss something between then and 2017?"

"Not really. In 2001, Tropical Storm Allison caused major Meyerland flooding. Five spec houses my grandfather built and sold to families on a street near the Bayou flooded. These people could barely scrape together their down payments and they certainly didn't have flood insurance. They lost everything. One tried to sue my grandfather, but lost. The destruction was from an act of God, not shoddy workmanship."

"That outcome makes sense."

"It did, but my grandfather still felt terrible. He'd convinced each of those families his ranch style homes were better buys than those in a subdivision just beyond Meyerland. They'd trusted him and in some perverse way, he thought his inattention to the bayou was a breach of that trust. Even though he'd been sued and won, he found a way to raise enough money that through a third party he bought back all five houses at a fair price so those families could start over."

"And then he built new houses?"

"No. My grandfather believed what goes around comes around. He bulldozed those five houses, made the area into a park, and donated it to the city."

"The park in the painting."

"Yes. It was dedicated after his death. Dad and Uncle Jack were running the company by then."

"Now I understand the sentimental value, but why didn't you report your painting when you originally missed it?"

She drained her drink and took a moment to swallow the olives. I waved to the waiter to bring us another round. Something didn't feel right, but I couldn't put my finger on it.

Olive flashed a smile at the waiter when he put her new drink, complete with two olives in front of her. She twirled the toothpick, stabbing the olives in the air. "If everyone got things right, like this martini, think how perfect life would be."

She bit the olives from the toothpick and savored them. "Because I assumed Daniel had it. You see, when we divorced, I gave him the house and whatever was in it except for certain personal things, which were to include that painting. Professional movers took my personal items to a storage unit while my mother and I went to Europe for eight months.

"The painting wasn't moved?"

"Apparently not."

I drummed my fingers on the bar. Olive stared at my hand until I stopped mid-beat. "Didn't you realize it was missing when you got back from Europe?"

"No. Until the day before Harvey, I never opened the storage unit." She shrugged. "By the time we returned from our trip, there wasn't anything in there I needed."

Now, it was her turn to move into my personal space. "I'm not one of those women in the stories you like to read. When I came back to the states, I consciously became an involved citizen and businesswoman living in the present. Daniel was in my past."

I let out a low whistle. This edgier side of Olive could be fun. "And I gather part of what Daniel offered when he showed up at your office was to paint your history for all to see?"

"That's right. Either underwrite his art or he'd see to it my family's secrets were displayed in an article interweaving art and events in Meyerland. Daniel's threats were veiled, but clear enough for me to understand. After he left, I confirmed my worst suspicions by going to the storage unit. If it hadn't been for Harvey, I would have tried to buy the painting back."

"By paying blackmail?"

She pressed her lips together in a tight line before relaxing enough to answer me. "A fair price, yes. Blackmail never."

"Murder?"

"Daniel was a skunk, but he was the kind of person who rose above the muck. He used his boat to save people while the storm raged, but he wouldn't have wanted his paintings wet. That's why he waited for a lull to retrieve them. If it wasn't raining or windy, how could he have been hit by falling or flying debris?"

She clenched her right hand into a fist, and then slowly released it. "Someone had to hit him."

"Positive it wasn't you or Uncle Jack?"

Olive grimaced. "Uncle Jack fixes things. At this stage in his life, he doesn't create bigger messes."

"And you?"

She reached over and rested her hand on my knee. "Harvey, I'm a Texas girl. Murder isn't my style."

I started to ask her what her style was, but they called my name to read my hurricane-driven noir poem. By the time I got back to my stool, she was gone. A fresh scotch sat on an unsigned check with enough zeroes to make me happy. I had a case to work on and the promise of some companions for the threads in my closet.

In the morning, despite a dull ache in my head, I was at the nearest non-flooded Harris County library when it opened. I figured with so many people lacking power, internet service, or having lost their computers like me, and at least four branch libraries closed indefinitely, computer access would be at a premium. I was right. Although I didn't feel great pushing my way past folks who might have had a rougher time than I did the past few days, I needed to verify what Olive had told me and as much as I could think of that she'd failed to mention.

After two hours, I understood her grandfather's reputation as a fair businessman was true, that early on, he'd brought his friend, Jack Griswald, into the business based upon a handshake, and that after her grandfather's death, Griswald and Olive's dad expanded Twist into the company it was today. Articles and pictures found through a Google search depicted Olive and her mother as blue-blood types—the kind who did charity work and attended debutante balls when they weren't busy being cheerleaders or marrying the team's football captain. Apparently, because Daniel Jones painted instead of playing football, a minimum of print space was devoted to his marriage to Olive.

I flipped through a lot of microfiche. A few articles depicted Daniel's rise as an artist and Olive's steady growth as part of Twist's management team. I didn't find any mention of their divorce or that either had remarried, but in later articles, another redhead, who I presumed was the bimbo, showed up in pictures from all of Daniel's openings. The picture captions made it clear she was his companion or date for the evening. The articles about Griswald were few and far between, but I knew from my one dealing with him that besides business, he loved art. Although I only learned about his painting stint from Olive, I was familiar with his extensive art collection. The job I'd done for him involved a title dispute for three paintings he donated to the local museum.

The last article I pulled up was the one Olive had shown me in the bar. I magnified it so I could see the painting's every detail. Viewing it closer, I realized how amateurish the painting was, which made me wonder more why Daniel had hung it where he did. I also realized that while the water line was below the painting, some of the flood water had lapped up onto it. There were places near the bottom where paint had flecked off.

Deciding my next move needed a visit with a cop friend of mine, I gave Andy a call. We met for lunch at the greasy spoon near the stationhouse.

When I told the waitress it would be one check, and I'd take it, Andy grunted his thanks. "It's not my birthday, so what's worth a free burger?"

"A little information about a redhead."

"Shoot."

"Ever hear of Olive Twist?"

"Who hasn't? She's pretty much the Twist conglomerate now that Jack Griswald has announced his impending retirement."

"Jack? What about her dad?" I bit into my medium-rare cheeseburger.

"He's around a few days a week, but he's always been a weak sister. Shortly before Old Man Twist died, he gave Griswald a large enough piece of the action to make sure the company would survive. With him in there, it thrived."

"Honestly?"

"Nah, but there wasn't anything we could ever prove. Olive's been his protégé. You involved with her? She's easy on the eyes. You going to eat that pickle?"

"You can have it." I handed him my sour pickle. "As for Olive, she's not my type. Her name came up in a conversation about Daniel Jones."

"That was a rotten loss for Houston. He was just coming into his own in the art world."

"Any idea who killed him?"

"We already released info about a limb or debris hitting him. You know something we should know?"

"Not a thing. The question raised is what's going to happen to his artwork. I understand there was quite a bit in his home and I figure he probably had some in his studio. Will the redhead he's been seeing get it?"

"No, he left a will. The art will go to his next of kin."

"Surviving children?"

"None that we can find." Andy peered over his glasses at me. "Everything goes to Olive Twist. From what we've pieced together, he never signed the divorce papers. They're still legally husband and wife. She can get the paintings anytime she wants. They aren't part of our investigation. How does that impact what you're working on?"

"It doesn't, but from what I've seen of her, you'd better inventory each one and make sure none are damaged. She's a stickler for things being just right."

For the rest of lunch, although I listened as he talked about the flooding, rescues and whatnot, I concentrated on my burger while planning what I wanted to say when I got to Olive's office after lunch.

After a little sparring with my client's secretary, she finally let Olive know that I was standing in her outer office and didn't plan to leave until I saw her. When Olive told her to bring me right in, I could tell the gatekeeper was miffed. Too bad. I was, too.

"Harvey, good to see you again. Won't you please sit down." She didn't rise, but pointed toward a conversation area with a leather couch and two chairs.

"I'll stand." I took the check out of my jacket pocket and lay it on her desk. "I think you need to sign this now."

Without saying anything, she pulled a pen from the marble desk set sitting in the middle of her mahogany desk and signed her name with a flourish. She replaced the pen, handed me the check, and pushed her chair back to where I could clearly see her legs. She crossed them. Once again, we engaged in our game of silence. Again, I cracked first.

"How do you get around signing things as Olive Twist when your married name is Jones?"

She pulled her skirt down and smoothed a wrinkle in it. "I never changed my name, so thankfully that wasn't a legal problem. You see, for all these years, until Daniel came to see me, I thought we were divorced. I had no idea he hadn't signed the papers."

"Most people get copies and put them away in case they need them in the future. Were your papers with the painting you thought was in your storage bin?"

"In a sense, yes. Harvey, I left the country and was gone for eight months. It was a tough time for me emotionally and well, I did a stupid thing. I relied on others to make sure the divorce was taken care of and my life would be back the way it was when, and if, I chose to come home."

I glanced around the office. There were no personal pictures of family members or pets. The décor was a deeper beige than the walls. I walked to the window and looked out. In the distance, I could see the park Olive said her grandfather had donated. It was beginning to make sense to me. "You considered living abroad?"

"Until I realized there was no need for me to stay away."

"Eight months is a long time." I waited, watching her stare at her hands. She wore no rings. "It would have been enough time to begin a new life."

"But that didn't happen." She looked up at me. I resisted wiping away the tear slithering down her cheek. "Our baby was stillborn."

"So, you came home and made a different life for yourself."

"Yes."

"Until Daniel threatened to tell people the truth about you, your grandfather and Jack?" I took her silence for an affirmation. "You went to Jack and told him what Daniel was threatening?"

Her head barely moved, but it was enough for me to put the final pieces together. "The police know you were never divorced. Daniel left a will leaving you everything. You can retrieve anything you want, but there may be a problem with Jack's painting. The flood peeled off some layers of paint near the bottom of the painting."

"That's no big deal. Like I told you, with grandfather gone and Uncle Jack aging, the painting reminds me of them when they were young. Call me sentimental."

I pocketed the check. "Me, too."

She didn't reply, but as I walked to her window, I imagined her Texas eyes followed me.

"You may need to use this view of the park to evoke those memories. By now, the police are checking out the picture underneath where the paint flecked. I'm pretty sure they're going to find Jack painted over the one your grandfather claimed was stolen. I understand when it wasn't recovered, the insurance company paid off exactly the sum used to buy out the five homeowners. As for Daniel, like you said, Uncle Jack was a fixer."

I left to cash my check, regretting I'd sworn off redheads.

* * *

Harvey and the Red-head is the first private detective story I wrote. It was published in The Eyes of Texas: Private Eyes from the Panhandle to the Piney Woods (Down & Out Books—October 2019). It was later read as a two-part podcast on Mystery Rat's Maze Podcast—Harvey and the Redhead Part 1 by Debra H. Goldstein (podbean.com) and Harvey and the Redhead Part 2 by Debra H. Goldstein (podbean.com).

Biff's Place

*Music soothes the soul, but with families and friends
like this family, it may also have other influences.*

Grand-Daddy swore music soothed the soul. His attitude and interpretation were purely clinical. He'd spent years in the university's lab playing music and seeing how it affected mood, blood pressure, and stroke recovery in mice and humans. If he'd lived a little longer, I could have told him about music's impact on murder and murderers.

I wonder what factors he would have considered. Perhaps gender, race, or family background? Maybe he would have added time and type of murder or weapon of choice. No matter how many elements he considered, knowing him, Grand-Daddy would have concluded the sampling was too small to be relevant.

That might have been the one time we disagreed. When it comes to murder, I believe a factor of one is sufficient for analysis. That's why my research, now that I work at the university, has veered in a different direction than his. He believed in examine, test, and repeat for certainty, while I lean more toward psychological profiling based upon human characteristics and how different emotional, environmental, and unpredicted events change outcomes.

Some have compared my research to shooting craps. It's doubtful my professional work would please Grand-Daddy, but I know he'd be thrilled if he could hear me jamming on my washboard Saturday nights at Biff's Place.

Grand-Daddy introduced me to Biff's Place in 1962, when I turned ten. Raising me after my parents died, he thought there were certain things that should be part of my education. Biff's Place was one of those things.

The first time he took me there, he told me "Ronnie, there are only a few juke joints like this left." I thought he meant in Mississippi, but he was referring to anywhere.

When he stopped chuckling, he continued his history lesson. "Juke joints were created in the South during the era of the Jim Crow laws, so black sharecroppers and plantation workers had a place to kick back after their long hours of work. Mr. Biff opened Biff's place almost twenty years ago with the idea that it would be a haven where race and social class would be ignored for the sake of the music."

"Have you been coming to this heaven since then?"

Again Grand-Daddy laughed. "I guess heaven is the right word. And yes, I have. Some of the best jazz and blues musicians play here, so I come to hear them. There's something about their music that I can't find in the lab."

He whistled as we drove through a neighborhood that had houses a lot smaller than his or the one where I used to live. Each time he turned on a street, I tried to read its sign. D Street was the last one I read before he said, "Here we are."

I glanced out the window, looking for the juke joint. I wasn't quite sure what it would look like, but I knew I didn't see it. The only things on D Street were a few rundown houses. The owner of one of them seemed to have tried to disguise its peeling paint by stringing a few Christmas lights across its roof and front doorway. Otherwise, it looked like any of the other two-story houses on the block.

"Where's the music place?"

"Right in front of you."

All I saw was the Christmas-light house and a lot next to it filled with cars.

"Are you sure we're on the right street?"

"Yes." He pointed toward the driveway.

My gaze followed the direction of his finger. This old house sure didn't look like the auditorium where Mama took me to see *The Nutcracker.*

"You're teasing me." I crossed my arms and didn't move.

"You'll see." He got out of the car, walked around to my side, opened my door, and offered me his hand. Still believing he was pulling my leg but not sure why, I took his hand and let him lead me down the gravel driveway.

I heard faint sounds ahead of us. About halfway down, I recognized the notes of a song. I didn't know what to think until we got to where the driveway wound behind the house, and there I saw musicians playing their hearts out under a tin roof that covered a three-walled wood platform that served as their stage. Even though I was only ten, it was at that moment I realized this might be Mr. Biff's home, but it was also something special. Not only were all types of people sitting at tables, enjoying the blues and jazz, but some were dancing with abandon on a small wooden dance floor set just below the front of the stage.

To this day, I remember staring at the people on and off the dance floor. My surprise and lack of understanding were all summed up by the tone in which I asked, "Grand-Daddy?"

"I told you it was a place for everyone to enjoy good music. They've also got great ribs. Want some?"

Before I could answer, he led me toward a big open fire with spits of meat turning above it. A man even larger and rounder than Grand-Daddy stood to its side, holding tongs and handing people ribs wrapped in aluminum foil. "Junior, this is my granddaughter Ronnie. Ronnie, this is Mr. Biff's son Junior."

He smiled at me. I was so fixated by his size and his beautiful midnight skin, I couldn't mumble anything except "thank you" when he handed me a foil-wrapped package. After thanking Junior more properly by paying him for my ribs, Grand-Daddy ushered me to a table on the far side of the dance floor. He opened the packet for me and, with jazz nourishing my soul, I bit into Junior's ribs. They were the best I'd ever tasted.

In between bites, a hand grasped my shoulder. I turned to see a slight man with a grin as wide as Junior's. For such a small person, his grip was strong. "You must be Ronnie. Your Grand-Daddy's mighty proud of you."

I looked from him to Grand-Daddy, not quite sure how to react. "Thank you, sir. I'm proud of him, too."

Apparently, this was my evening to amuse grown-ups, because both Grand-Daddy and the man laughed. "You should be."

"Now, Biff," Grand-Daddy said. Realizing this must be Mr. Biff, I snuck a quick peek at Grand-Daddy. He looked pleased as punch.

I guess he was so excited that his manners went out the window because he didn't introduce me to Mr. Biff. Instead, I took matters into my own hands. I thrust my sticky hand out at Mr. Biff. He shook it.

"Pleased to meet you Mr. Biff. Grand-Daddy said your place is like heaven and that he enjoys coming here, so I'm sure I will, too."

"Well, let's see that you do. Come with me."

I glanced at Grand-Daddy for permission. His nod was almost imperceptible, but it was a yes. With Grand-Daddy staying behind, Mr. Biff led me through the dance floor to the stage. My forty-two pounds didn't seem to matter to him as he swung me onto the stage. He scrambled up beside me and said something to the two guitarists already sitting there.

Leaning over to where a group of instruments lay, Mr. Biff picked up two washboards. He handed me the smaller one, plus a wooden spoon, and then put metal thimbles on his fingers. "Ronnie, when I nod to you, I want you to hit your spoon against your washboard. Understand?"

I don't know if he heard my whispered "yes," because the guitarists began playing. Holding his washboard to his chest, Mr. Biff tapped and scraped his metal board, complementing the beat, much like a drum. Periodically, he nodded to me and I diligently struck my spoon against my washboard. When we finished the number, everyone applauded. I left the stage in a cloud of euphoria.

It was a high that I haven't often achieved since then. In the years since my first visit, Grand-Daddy passed, I've grown up, and the world and politics have changed, but not the atmosphere at Biff's Place. It's still going strong every Saturday night. Oh, and Junior's ribs are still the best in town.

There have been some changes, though. Not all of them to my liking. Somewhere in the last decade, Mr. Biff has stopped sitting to the side of the stage, playing at least one set where he improvised beautiful guitar riffs. Instead, he has settled into using his guitar or slide trombone to warm up the crowd, or when the other musicians take a break. Most evenings, he simply works the crowd—welcoming everyone. Whether he clasps a hand, smiles, or poses for a photograph with an out-of-town guest, Mr. Biff is still the heart of Biff's Place.

There's talk he's slacking off because he's given up some of the administrative duties, like setting the lineup for the acts or collecting money, but he's earned the right. After all, he's ninety-two now.

For his ninetieth birthday and the celebration honoring forty years of Biff's Place, the local paper sent out a young reporter to do an article commemorating both. I happened to sit with them during the interview, so I heard how the cub tried to find a way to sensationalize his story.

Mr. Biff wasn't having any of it.

When the reporter tried stirring something up by commenting on integration and the dance floor, Mr. Biff cut him off. "We don't have no color here. If you bring a bottle of wine or a couple of beers and pay your ten dollars, you're welcome to grab a seat, mosey around, or dance the night away. People come here for the music, but if you get hungry, you can get an order of BBQ ribs from my son."

Trying a different tactic, the young man observed that Mr. Biff let newcomers sit in with established players. Surely, the reporter said, "that isn't fair to patrons who pay their cover charge expecting to hear only name talent."

That one absolutely made Mr. Biff guffaw. When he finally got himself under control, he stared at the kid. "How else they going to know what greatness is? They not only learn from the masters, but they don't want to be shown up, so they go home and practice twice as hard."

Mr. Biff not only believed in practice and learning from the best, but he was adamant that he wouldn't put up with any nonsense at Biff's Place. He'd seen his share of drugs and other such in the music world and had decided that wasn't going to be tolerated at Biff's Place. People weren't there to do drug deals, carouse, or start fights. To quote my Grand-Daddy misquoting some politician, "It's the music, stupid."

At least it was from the forties through the seventies. The seventies brought a new generation of neighbors to D Street and the surrounding neighborhood. These folks weren't as educated about Biff's Place and its cultural significance. Instead, they complained about the cars, traffic, and noise. A few brought their issues directly to Mr. Biff, but when his response didn't satisfy them, they took it to County Sheriff Thomas Jefferson Riley.

Better known as T.J., the sheriff has never been one to turn a blind eye to a problem. That's why, by 1970, he'd been repeatedly elected county sheriff. The last time, the other party didn't even run a candidate against him. They knew T.J. was in it for the long haul, and that, in Mississippi, there's no set limit to the number of years a sheriff can serve.

As he did with any citizen's complaint, T.J. apparently listened sympathetically and promised to do something about the cars roaming the neighborhood looking for Biff's Place. Understanding the optics of pleasing folks, he did. T.J. immediately had big signs made with arrows and words pointing the way to Avenue D and Biff's Place.

The next Saturday night he rode through the neighborhood, stopping here and there to post the signs. T.J. was so efficient that he was always right on time for his weekly saxophone solo at Biff's Place.

He'd been playing there for years, but most people, unless they frequented Biff's Place often, didn't realize it because T.J. was white, and back then, blacks and whites seldom sat down together. But behind the scenes, the magic of music broke those barriers.

Until Grand-Daddy died, he, T.J., and Mr. Biff were tight. I remember Grand-Daddy observing that T.J. was Mr. Biff's son from another mother. While T.J. might make some noise here and there, it was a safe bet he would never shut Biff's Place down.

The signs didn't stop people from crowding the street, parking on the edge of yards, or making noise, but they proved T.J. had responded to the public's complaints.

I saw the signs, but I didn't pay much attention to them. I wasn't going by Biff's Place as often as I had in the past. Even if the summer of 1970 hadn't been the kind where the sweltering Mississippi heat took care of the need for any kind of cover or clothes at night, I was, at eighteen, so hot to trot, I didn't need to look at a thermometer. I'd found the one special boy, Cooper "Skip" Carter, with whom I wanted to spend the rest of my life.

Mr. Biff didn't like him.

That was okay with us. My twenty-two-year-old love didn't care to spend Saturday evenings at Biff's Place anyway. His music tastes ran more to hard metal than jazz or blues.

Coming from the way Grand-Daddy had raised me, Skip's bad-boy image excited me.

"Look," he'd told me. "I bounced in and out of college and got into trouble for some stupid pranks." He rubbed his left thumb against the second and third fingers of his hand. "Luckily, my old man had the bank account to make that crap go away."

One of the nights we were riding around in his truck, I mentioned how close Mr. Biff, T.J., and Grand-Daddy had been. Skip frowned and spat out the window. "I did a stint in rehab last year because of our no-good local sheriff."

"T.J.?"

"Yeah, him. He didn't like my friends, always hassling them and hassling me just because I was with them. One time he arrested us for drug possession, but he couldn't prove I had anything on me. He charged me just the same, then convinced my father that a stint in rehab would be the best way for me to walk away with a clean record. I don't blame the old man for thinking rehab was better than a chance of probation or jail time, but T.J.'s at the top of my shit list. All those sessions examining who I really am were the biggest pile of garbage imaginable. The only benefit of that place was I learned a lot of practical things, including who I can trust."

He kissed me and I melted. So what if he'd been a wild child? It was all behind him. Once this summer ended, Skip planned to start a two-year program at our local community college before transferring to Ole Miss.

I was ecstatic. We'd be in lock step at the junior college, where I was going to work toward an associate degree. Until I'd met Skip, I'd assumed I'd follow the traditional route from junior college to a four-year school to receive a college degree. It was something Grand-Daddy had encouraged before he died. But who knew now? Where would our dreams take us?

Lying entwined in bed, we often talked about making a future together. One thing Skip wanted to do was travel. "You know," he said, "we're at an age that if we put off school for a year, we could see the world fairly cheaply by staying at youth hostels. You've never been to Europe, have you?"

"I've never been out of Mississippi."

He let go of me and propped himself up on our pillows. "Then, that's what we need to do. The Alps in Switzerland, gondola rides and The Leaning Tower of Pisa in Italy, and, of course, Paris, the city of love. Doesn't that sound wonderful?"

It did. I was sure Grand-Daddy would have understood that four years is a long time to wait when you're in love. We decided to go in the fall, but in the meantime, we vowed to make the most of our summer in Mississippi.

Trips to the lake, picnics, odd jobs for him, and a schedule of sleeping in and staying up late made the days and nights speed by. The only time Skip left my side was for an occasional day of squirrel or raccoon hunting—the two animals Mississippi legally allowed him to shoot in the summer. On those days, I prayed he'd come home empty-handed. Neither the idea of his shooting an animal, even a squirrel or raccoon, nor the idea of eating it sat well with me.

Skip tried to interest me in hunting with him, but when that didn't work, he suggested shooting might be something we could do together. Going to the dresser, he pulled out a pistol like those I'd seen on TV.

"I didn't know you had a gun in there."

He gently rubbed the gun's shiny chrome finish. "This is my pride and joy. It's a Colt 1911 .45 caliber."

"Please be careful. It looks like it could go off easily."

"Relax. This baby has a feather trigger, but the safety is on."

Even if the safety was on, I wasn't comfortable with the way Skip casually handled his gun. The tension in my shoulders only eased when he put it back into the drawer.

As the summer progressed, we rock 'n' rolled along, avoiding blues and jazz. Everything was perfect as we made our plans for the fall. Perfect that is until Skip came home agitated and out of sorts after a day of hunting.

Hoping to relax him, I rubbed his back. After a few minutes, his mood seemed to lighten. "Better?"

He turned toward me, put his hand under my chin, and raised my face to see his clearly. "You're right, babe. No need to be gloomy. Let's go out and have ourselves a night on the town. Put on that pretty dress of yours and we'll have dinner at Joe's."

For a moment I thought about the special chicken cacciatore dinner I'd planned for us, but seeing Skip's eagerness to please me, I agreed.

"Give me a minute to change and put away what I have in the oven."

"Sure thing." Skip leaned over, kissed me, and mumbled something about an appetizer.

We left for dinner a little later than we'd planned. While I got in the front seat of the truck, he grabbed two beers out of a Styrofoam cooler on the floor of the backseat. Getting in next to me, he made a grand gesture of twisting the cap off the first and handing it to me. As I giggled at his formality, Skip opened the second and drank half in one swig.

I raised my eyebrows.

"It's okay, babe. I've got this under control."

I snuggled closer to him.

He turned up the volume on his radio. A few minutes later, Skip turned the car into the almost-empty parking lot of a convenience store a couple of blocks from Biff's Place.

I raised my head from his shoulder.

"Sorry, I need to make a quick business call before we go to dinner." Skip pointed to the pay phone at the end of the building. "Stay in the car. This will only take a moment."

"But—"

"Don't worry. I'll leave the motor and radio on. Plus, you'll have my special friend with you." He reached under the seat and pulled out the gun he'd shown me in our bedroom a few weeks earlier. I knew Skip usually kept his hunting rifle secured in the back of his truck, but I had no idea this pistol was hidden here, too.

"Isn't it illegal to have that in here?"

"You worry too much."

He flicked something on the side of the gun then handed it to me.

I took it carefully. "The safety?"

"I don't want you having to deal with that if you need it. This baby's cocked and locked, ready to fire. You'll be okay while I make my call." When Skip slammed the door, I stared at the gun, frightened the jarring bang might set it off.

Grand-Daddy had taught me lots of things, but guns were never in his lesson plans. One part of me wanted to put the pistol down, while the other counted the seconds for Skip to return and take it from me.

Hearing a voice shouting, I gingerly, lest I moved too fast because the gun's safety was still off, glanced around the parking lot. The person yelling stood in the store's doorway.

"Turn that racket off or get out of here before I call the police!"

Afraid to reach for the radio knob, I didn't respond, but neither did Skip, who was talking on the phone, his body turned away from the man in the doorway. After a few seconds, the man turned and went back inside the store.

Skip was still on his call. Finally, he hung up and sauntered back to the truck.

He slid behind the steering wheel and slammed it with the palm of his hand, his gaze scanning the parking lot.

"Let's go, please. The man in the store said if we didn't turn down the music, he'd call the police."

Skip hit the steering wheel again. "Not now. Just sit there and be quiet. There's some business I have to take care of first."

With my head, I motioned toward the gun. "Don't you want to put this back under the seat?"

"In a minute. I might need it."

"What?"

"Only kidding. Lighten up a bit." He hushed as a car entered the parking lot. It drove toward us, blinking its lights once. When our lights went off and then back on, I realized that Skip had responded. The other car drove up next to us, driver to driver, making it easy for the drivers to talk.

Without a word, the other driver held up a clear plastic bag. Skip nodded and reached under his seat again. I flinched, waiting to see if he had another gun. Instead, he pulled out a brown paper bag. When Skip partially opened the bag to expose its contents to the other driver, I could see the bag was filled with money.

Just like that, the bags were switched, the exchange completed. Skip casually dropped the plastic bag on the seat between us. As a few pills escaped onto the seat, the other driver backed up and sped out of the parking lot.

We sat there, our music still blaring. The same man again came out of the store, threatening to call the police if we didn't turn down the music.

Skip laughed. He flipped a bird at the man but showed no inclination to move. The screamer went back inside the store.

"Please, let's do what he asked or let's go." I looked down at my trembling hands, which still held the gun, and willed them to stop moving.

"All in good time. It drives him crazy to have music blaring in his parking lot."

"You've done this before?" I didn't need an answer. I didn't know the man I was sitting next to. Still holding the gun, I reached for the car door handle as a police car came into the parking lot. It parked near the entrance of the store.

"Where do you think—" Skip yanked me back into the truck and took the gun from my hand as the driver climbed out of the police car. It was T.J.

Instead of going into the store, T.J. walked across the lot in our direction, his hand resting on his holster. "Hey, there," he called. "Turn down the music, please."

I reached for the radio's button, but Skip swatted my hand.

"Come on, Skip. Let's get out of here."

"I don't think so. I'm tired of that pig always putting his nose into my business. Maybe it's time to teach him a lesson." He trained the gun on T.J.

"Skip, no!"

"Be quiet."

Ignoring me huddled in the seat next to him, Skip waited, chanting, "Bang, Bang, you're going to be dead." I tried to warn T.J., but only a squeak came out of my mouth. Even if I had been able to yell, I doubt T.J. would have heard me, but the man sitting next to me did. He stopped aiming his gun long enough to slap me and say, "Shut up."

Cowering, I couldn't silence a soft whimper.

His hand darted at me again, but by now, I was just outside his reach.

T.J. approached the truck, repeating his suggestion to turn down the music. Skip didn't answer.

It was only when T.J.'s eyes and mouth opened in surprise as he simultaneously stared down the barrel of the gun and began to duck, that I reacted. I brought my left hand down hard against Skip's arm, much like a karate chop I'd seen on television. The sound of a blast, a scream and silence filled my ears.

I sat still, absorbing the slack of his jaw, empty eyes, and the red splotch spreading across his stomach. I started to reach across the seat, hoping to slow the flow, when T.J. opened the passenger door and stopped me.

"He needs help."

"Not now."

T.J. pulled me from the car. "Come on. Get over to Biff's Place. Go in through the front door. It's unlocked."

"What?" In all the years I'd gone to Biff's Place, I'd never been in his house beyond the downstairs bathroom in the back that he let everyone use.

"Ronnie, hush. Just do what I'm telling you to do. I'll try to call Mr. Biff and warn him you're coming, but if I don't get him, wait in the kitchen. He'll come in to cool off between sets. Tell him I said to clean you up and get you on stage with your washboard."

I stared at him. "But…"

"Do it. Now!"

Without another word, I followed his instructions. I ran the two blocks like the wind. I found Mr. Biff already in the kitchen. He led me to a chair and without a word he washed my hands and face. "Take off your blouse."

"What?"

"You've got blood on it." I glanced down and saw blood spatter on my shirt. I fought the urge to retch by focusing on easing out of my shirt and sliding into the Biff's Place T-shirt that Mr. Biff handed me.

"Stand up."

I did as I was told.

"You'll do. Now, come on." Still carrying my blouse and the washcloth, now wadded into a ball, he led me outside. "Get on stage, grab a washboard and jam. Make it fancy."

Again, I followed directions, but I never took my eyes off Mr. Biff as he walked up to Junior and his flaming pit. He said something to Junior and then, taking one of the sticks I'd seen Junior use in preparing his ribs, I saw Mr. Biff drop my shirt and the washcloth into the fire. He poked and prodded at it. From the leap of the flames, I gathered he'd made sure there would be no trace of either.

Looking away, I concentrated on making my washboard sing. When we finished the number, everyone applauded. Although somewhat calmed by the music, I didn't take the lead again for the rest of the evening, I stayed on the stage until T.J. arrived, and he and Mr. Biff motioned me off.

The next few days were a blur. T.J. took me back to the apartment to gather my few belongings, and he found me another place to stay. After the local newspaper learned about the methamphetamine in Skip's system and about the hundreds of diet pills found in his truck—diet pills back then included meth as an appetite suppressant—they spun my lover's story as being that of a kid who went to rehab, came home, relapsed, and put himself out of his own misery. No one questioned their conclusion.

There was a mention or two that I'd been seen around town with the deceased, but it faded because, with Mr. Biff and T.J.'s help, I went straight to Ole Miss instead of the junior college. By the time I came home, degrees in hand, not many remembered the incident. Instead, they all were too busy remarking on the cute love of my life, my son. I think Grand-Daddy would also have loved him and understood why now I study how people behave and whether the traits of killers can be inherited.

* * *

Given a choice between writing about juke joints or honky tonks, my adopted Southern ways won out in this story published in Jukes & *Tonks: Crime Music Inspired by Music in the Dark and Suspect Choices (Down & Out Books – 2021).*

Grandma's Garden

There are moments in families that truth, lies, and tears mix to a point that they can't be straightened out for years.

My grandmother told me rain makes flowers grow, the warning flags at the beach are changed from white to red by elves, and "your father loves you." It took me years to figure out her lies.

Grandma was not like a touch of soft fabric or the smell of just baked cookies. The scratchy feel of her cheeks was similar to her mothering. I've come to realize it couldn't have been easy for her to raise a scrawny kid in the condo where my father stuck us. No easier than it was for her to trade her garden for window boxes sitting on a cement patio. Back then, watching her cook, clean, or get me ready for school, it was hard for me to associate her with Dad. Housedresses and jogging suits didn't match the red-carpet tuxedoed pictures of him I cut from magazines. Maybe that's why he didn't visit often.

Don't get me wrong. A beachfront condo and open charge cards let me grow up loving sunrises and sunsets, running in the surf, and having a perpetual tan. Much as I loved the white-grained sand of our beach, Grandma would have preferred soil for her garden. Before Dad moved Grandma and me to the beach, she had a real yard in which she grew tomatoes, sunflowers, and herbs in a design layout only she understood. Neither he nor I paid much attention when she explained how her plant placement was tied to sunshine and shade, and how the slope of the land puddled rain. To us, her garden was a hodgepodge.

We were in the condo a week when we received a Homeowners Association notice that condo regulations prohibited planting in the patch outside our door. We received a second cease and desist letter complaining about the wood boxes Grandma attached to our front windows. Dad called after his secretary received a copy of our third citation. Grandma assured Dad she would take care of the situation and then went and made herself a cup of tea. She was sitting on our patio when she decided that if no one objected to outdoor chairs, tables, or grills, the watchdogs couldn't complain about window boxes sitting on the cement. They didn't.

Grandma planted, weeded, and even staked tomato plants in those window boxes. I was the assigned watergirl. Twice a day, I checked each box to see if the soil was moist or sunbaked. Because she didn't like the concentrated pressure of water from a hose, if the soil was too dry, she would make me take our metal watering can, fill it, and sprinkle from high up so the plants would think it was rain.

"Plants don't have brains," I said, trickling water over a new flat of pansies. "Why try to fool them when they can't figure out the trick?"

"You're not tricking them. They know what you're doing." She turned a box to expose its other side to the sun.

"Wouldn't it soak everything better if I use the hose?"

"Maybe," she said, pushing back her sunhat, "but think about how petals sip each free falling droplet when it rains."

Until last April's hurricane swept our patio clean, I kept Grandma's garden growing after her death. Now, watching a lifeguard change the red flags to white, my tears fall like rain.

* * *

Grandma's Garden received a Mobile Pensters Prize and an Alabama Writers Conclave Award. It was originally published in www.Alalit.com *(2014) and reprinted by Texas Gardener,* **SEEDS** *(January 21, 2015). A modified version of the story appeared in the 2012 short story anthology,* **It Was a Dark and Stormy Night.**

Forensic Magic

*The magic of childhood—even when tinged
by sin—protects the path of the future.*

Ten minutes earlier, everything seemed magical. Lights twinkled, music played, people danced in the open area near the Watch Hill Flying Horse Carousel. Little kids trailed the clown making balloon animals while their parents waited in a line curling down Bay Street for a reading by the fortune teller.

A group of older women, members of the ladies auxiliary who'd made and served all the food for our 1953 Summertime church bazaar dinner, sat fanning themselves at tables set up in the grassy area next to the wood-framed pavilion that housed the carousel. Some sipped lemonade. A few took off their shoes and, while carefully holding their skirts tightly to their legs, rested their feet on empty chairs. They were taking a break for the hour before Pastor Smith, who was new to our church, began the highlight of the evening —the pie auction.

With two bits in my pocket, I probably was more excited than anyone else about this evening's fun because, now that I was twelve, Daddy was allowing me to bid for a slice of pie. The only problem, the way I saw it, was there might be a delay starting the auction. Pastor Smith was lying dead on the ground behind the pavilion.

It didn't seem real, but I knew it was true. I was the one who found him.

Normally, no one, especially me, would have left the square during the bazaar, but when you gotta go, you gotta go, and the only nearby options were in use. Desperate, I went behind the pavilion hoping to find an out of the way tree. I was cutting back toward the stage area to watch The Ocean Staters, a group of guys who dropped out of the Community College of Rhode Island hoping to make it big in the music world, play their second set when I saw something in the grass partially blocking the dirt path. It was Pastor Smith.

I tried to scream, but nothing came out. For a second, I shut my eyes. When I opened them again, the pastor still lay there. For a moment I thought about running to get my dad, but my curiosity took over. I inched forward, but not too close. From the way he was lying with his eyes glazed over, mouth open, and a few flies resting on the shaft of the knife stuck in his chest, I knew he was beyond Daddy or me helping him.

Most twelve-year-olds would have been too frightened to do anything; but, having spent hours poring over the *Magic of Forensic Science* book that came with my mail order detective kit, my training took over. Realizing this was my first real investigation, I backed up and walked in a large circle around the spot where Pastor Smith lay. I was careful because, like the book said, I didn't want to disturb the crime scene while I looked for clues.

The ground was soft from last night's rain, but I didn't see any obvious footprints or anything the killer had dropped, so I moved closer to him. Other than the knife and a big bloodstain on his shirt, nothing caught my eye until I glanced at the ground where he lay. There were a few round holes or indentations in the dirt and some dime sized drops of red that looked like they might be blood trailed into the grass. Had someone with a cane, umbrella, or pole stood near the pastor before stabbing him? What had he done to make someone mad enough to kill him?

Even though my book said forensic science was the magic of the future to solve cases, I couldn't think of anything from the book that answered my questions. It was time to get Daddy. After all, he's our town's sheriff.

Coming back to the square through the grass, I tried to steer clear of the auxiliary ladies as I looked around for Daddy. They always want to talk to me about how much I've grown and there wasn't time for that today. But even from where I stood, there was no misunderstanding the loud voices of the co-presidents, Bertha Tuttle and Karen Johnson. I couldn't help glancing in their direction.

Mrs. Tuttle and Mrs. Johnson were complaining about Pastor Smith and the changes he was making.

"After all these years, he wants to do away with the pie auction," Mrs. Tuttle said.

Mrs. Johnson stopped fanning herself and leaned forward. "But that's not the only auxiliary project Pastor Smith wants us to end. Right after we finished cutting up the corn bread for tonight, he had the audacity, while grabbing a piece, to tell Bertha and me that in his opinion the auxiliary puts too much work into the bazaar for the money we raise. I thought he was going to pat me on the head when he suggested we should defer to the proposals he and the men's fundraising committee will introduce at the board meeting next month."

Mrs. Tuttle crossed her arms over her ample chest. "Do you know what he suggested we do?" I was used to hearing her speak, but as she rushed her words, her voice became far louder. "Start a sewing guild and, of course, continue baking our brownies and other goodies for the church's weekly fellowship hour." She narrowed her eyes. "You know, I bet he didn't vote for Ike."

"Bertha calm down," Mrs. Johnson said. "You're all flushed. It doesn't matter who he or anyone else voted for. You know how it goes: men talk, women work. There's no chance the good pastor will get his way. We'll be here long after him."

Not wanting to call attention to myself, I stopped eavesdropping and walked closer to the dancers and peered around the square again. I finally spotted my father. He was making nice to Miss Meghan, Mrs. Johnson's daughter, by the table where the pies were displayed.

She's the first lady since Mom died three years ago who Daddy has paid any attention to. They were both smiling as she showed him one of the pies. I guess Daddy was making sure he bought the right one this year. It was going to cost him a pretty penny because not only were Miss Meghan's pies known to be some of the best, but Daddy wasn't the only man who had an interest in her.

"Daddy, come with me." I tugged his sleeve.

"Where's your manners, boy? Can't you see I'm talking to an adult?"

"Yes, sir." I dropped my hand from his jacket. "Good-evening Miss Meghan."

She gave me that smile adults give children who are interrupting them. I ignored it and stepped closer to my father. "Daddy, I'm sorry, but this is important."

The look Daddy gave me meant I'd be in trouble later and that I'd better stop pestering him now, but thankfully Miss Meghan intervened. "Les, you better go see what that boy wants. If it's that important—"

"It is."

"Well then, I'm going to get a lemonade and sit myself down to listen to the music. My Mama and the other auxiliary ladies put so much effort into getting everything just right, despite having to deal with last night's rain and Pastor Smith getting in their way, that they're worn out. I know he's new to the community and how we do things, but I could have killed him for getting my mother and Mrs. Tuttle so upset today." Miss Meghan nodded in the direction where the ladies sat. "When you finish with Toby, you'll come find me, won't you?"

"I sure will. Shouldn't be but a few minutes. Why don't you get me a lemonade, too, please?"

Daddy sounded pleasant enough, but I could tell from how carefully he spoke each word that what I needed better be good, or else. The moment Miss Meghan sauntered away from us, he turned toward me. "Well?"

"It's Pastor Smith. He's lying dead behind the carousel pavilion."

"He's what?"

"Lying with a knife in his chest behind the pavilion. Based upon my

Magic of Forensic Science book, I didn't think you'd want a lot of people messing up the crime scene before you had a chance to look it over."

Daddy let me lead him quickly across the square. Even though we didn't stop walking, I saw Daddy scan the crowd. Without him telling me, I knew he was looking for Uncle Evan.

It wasn't hard to spot him. Uncle Evan was the only one on the square dressed as a clown. Catching his eye, Daddy signaled him to join us. After a final twist and knotting of a balloon dog Uncle Evan was making for a little girl, he did.

Uncle Evan isn't my real uncle or a real clown. He's Daddy's deputy. Uncle Evan and his wife, Adele, who today was telling fortunes for five cents each, have been in my life since I was a baby. I've always called them Uncle and Aunt. Since Mom died, Aunt Adele has taken care of me a lot while Daddy and Uncle Evan worked.

"What is it, Les?" Uncle Evan matched our stride.

"Toby says we have a body on our hands."

"A what?"

By now we were rounding the corner to the back of the pavilion. I pointed toward the crumpled brown pile with the silver knife standing up from it.

"Who is it?"

Daddy didn't have to answer because once they reached the body, it was obvious it was Pastor Smith. As Daddy began circling the area exactly as I'd done, Uncle Evan plunged forward and reached his hand out to touch Pastor Smith.

"Wait," I said. "You don't want to disturb any forensic evidence."

Uncle Evan stopped. He came back to me. Leaning over, he touched my ear and pulled a quarter out of it. He handed it to me. "Why don't you go get yourself a soda or ice cream and let us tend to this?"

When Daddy didn't object, I took the quarter. I hadn't seen Uncle Evan put his hand in his pocket or do anything that could explain the trick, but his type of magic didn't interest me as much as what they might discover examining the body. Knowing I was being shooed away, I complied for a step or two. That was enough to satisfy Uncle Evan that I was leaving. He turned back toward where Daddy was now bent on his knees next to Pastor Smith.

Quietly, I came closer so I could be Daddy and Uncle Evan's fly on the wall.

"There's no sign of a struggle," Daddy said. "The grass doesn't appear to be disturbed."

I was surprised. Had Daddy read my book while I was sleeping? "No footprints, but Evan what do you make of these holes in the ground near the body?"

"Not sure. Maybe they were there."

Daddy rubbed his chin as he stared at them. When Daddy pointed out the few round red spots in the grass and said he thought they might be blood, I felt quite pleased with my powers of observation.

"How long do you think he's been here?" Uncle Evan asked.

Daddy didn't immediately answer him, but I couldn't help myself. I could picture the page in my book on rigor mortis and I was proud to use the knowledge I'd gained from my mail order studies. "At least four hours. Rigor mortis sets in from four hours to four days from death."

"Toby?"

My gaze met Daddy's. His eyes were widened in surprise. His look and silence encouraged me to keep helping him.

I glanced at my watch. "Assuming he's been dead for four hours, at a minimum, that means he was killed when people started setting up the bazaar or sometime just before then." I raised my hand to hush Uncle Evan, who seemed ready to politely tell me to get lost.

Daddy put his hand on my shoulder "That's good thinking, son. I think you're right about when he was killed. Based upon that forensic book you've been studying, is there anything else that pops into your mind?"

Biting my lip, I thought hard. Daddy was giving me a chance to pull a rabbit out of my hat with all the stuff I'd been reading, but nothing was jumping out at me. I wished some brilliant thought would come to me with the same ease of magic Uncle Evan had pulled the quarter from my ear. Silently, I ran through the chapters in the book and then it hit me.

"Daddy, in the book's introduction, there's a story taken from the first book ever written about pathology. Apparently back in the 13th century, someone was killed and the person investigating the crime used an animal carcass to try out various weapons he thought might have made the wound. After figuring out the weapon probably was a sickle, he had everyone from the area bring their sickles to one location. When the smell of blood caused flies to gather on one sickle, like the flies are doing here, he knew who the murderer was. Everyone thought he'd solved the case using some spell to bring the flies to the sickle, but it was really forensic magic."

"But that doesn't help us," Uncle Evan said. "We've got the knife and flies but no one holding the weapon. There might be some fingerprints on the knife, but that will take us some time to nail down."

"True," I replied, "but the killer left us something different that we can use now."

I pointed to the small round indentations Daddy had mentioned and the spots on the grass that both he and I had observed. "The ground wasn't hard enough for footprints, but I've been thinking what could have made those holes. When Daddy agreed that the red spots on the grass are blood, it hit me."

"Well?" Daddy waited for me to explain myself.

For a moment I relished my first success as a detective using forensic magic to solve a case. "All the women at the bazaar are wearing heels. While stabbing Pastor Smith, the killer's heels would have gotten stuck in the soft dirt. Each time she pulled her heel out of the ground, she left a hole. When she walked away on the grass, the little spots left were made from blood she got on the bottom of her heels."

From Daddy's smile and the way he patted me on my back, I knew what I'd said made sense. "Evan, call the coroner and make sure everything is kept. Toby and I need to get back out to the square before the auction takes place."

I looked at my watch again. We only had about nine minutes until auction time.

Uncle Evan looked down at his clown suit. "Les?"

"No problem. The coroner won't care. In the meantime, Toby and I are going to add a new dimension to this year's auction."

I wasn't sure what Daddy was thinking, but as he explained his plan, I was thrilled it included me. Still, I was concerned. "Daddy, did I miss something?"

"Nope, you nailed it." He reached into his pocket for his wallet. Opening it, Daddy removed a twenty. "We're going to let all the women have a chance to win this before the auction begins."

And that's exactly what Daddy did. He strolled to the stage where The Ocean Staters were finishing up and grabbed the microphone. "Before we have the auction, we're going to have a special-ladies only game where each of you will have a chance to win something special." Daddy held up the bill so everyone could see it. "$20."

That caught everyone's attention—male and female, but Daddy repeated it was a ladies only event.

"Why is it for the ladies only?" someone shouted.

"Isn't it obvious? It's a thanks for everything our ladies auxiliary did to make this a perfect bazaar. Now, if each of you ladies will take off your shoes and put them in front of the bandstand, we'll begin the game."

While The Ocean Staters softly played *Blue Suede Shoes*, Daddy jokingly picked his way through the shoes, making comments about each one as he turned them over. As he did that, I scouted around to see who hadn't taken her shoes off.

There were three women. I tried being funny when I yelled to Daddy that Miss Meghan, Mrs. Tuttle, and Mrs. Johnson weren't playing the game. Daddy was much smoother than me as he worked his way over to their table.

"Now, ladies, everyone else is participating."

"Les, Mama and Mrs. Tuttle are too tired to play," Miss Meghan said softly.

"Well, then I will play for them." With a dramatic swoop, Daddy got down on one knee. He picked up Miss Meghan's foot and examined the bottom of her shoe. She giggled but went along with his Prince Charming patter.

Not looking as happy with his elegant gestures and references to Cinderella, Miss Meghan's mother waved him away as she leaned back in her chair, resting her feet up on the one in front of her. "Sheriff, I'm too tired to play."

With a final glance in Mrs. Johnson's direction, Daddy turned to Mrs. Tuttle. Her response was more insistent. "Sheriff, this isn't funny. I don't think it's proper for you to be touching my feet."

Daddy didn't argue with her. He stood and handed me the twenty. "Toby, go grab any shoe and give its owner the $20 prize." I nodded and started to scoot back toward the grandstand but stopped when I heard him tell Mrs. Tuttle he knew she'd done it. I stared at Mrs. Tuttle and Daddy.

"Les, what are you talking about?" Miss Meghan asked.

Daddy kept his gaze focused on Mrs. Tuttle's face. "Mrs. Tuttle, you and Pastor Smith got into it, right?"

She looked at the ground.

He bent again and gently lifted her foot. "The evidence is on your shoe."

Mrs. Tuttle held her hands out in front of her. "It was an accident. Karen and I had finished cutting the corn bread when he told us this would be the last bazaar. While Karen was putting up the cornbread, I followed him behind the pavilion to try to talk some sense into him. I still had the knife in my hand. When he started saying the times are changing and it's time to move on from old ideas and let younger people take over, we got into it."

She paused and looked at her hands, which were frozen in mid-air.

"I was talking with my hands. I do that when I get upset, like now. The pastor got too close and … I don't know how it happened, but suddenly I realized he'd been stabbed."

I turned at the whoosh sound that both Miss Meghan and her mother made, but Daddy kept his gaze on Mrs. Tuttle. "You'll have to come with me now," he said.

That night, when Daddy came in to tell me goodnight, he asked to see my mail order detective stuff, including my *Magic of Forensic Science* book. I picked the book up from my nightstand and handed it to him. He turned it over and read the back cover. "I see they have a second book in the series. Let's order it tomorrow."

Those two books still sit on the shelf in my office. Every now and then, since I replaced my father as sheriff, I consult them.

* * *

Forensic Magic was included in Masthead: Best New England Crime Stories (Level Best Books – December 2020).

A Corn Puddin' Wedding

Food, holidays, and murder have a nasty way of mixing and leaving a mark forever.

"As soon as you finish the marrying part, we're gonna have cake."

"Only cake?" Judge Ingram stared at Tommy and Melinda, the younger siblings of the couple whose wedding he'd be officiating within the next hour. He figured they were about eight or nine years old. "How about pumpkin pie, too? After all, this is a Thanksgiving themed wedding."

Tommy paused for a minute, chewing on a nail already bitten to the quick. He took his finger from his mouth and put the damp digit between his neck and the starched collar of his shirt. The judge noticed the boy's shirt still had creases from being in its plastic wrapping. "Cake," Tommy said. "My pa said this is like a big birthday party. So, there's going to be cake and…"

"Tommy!" the pig-tailed girl interrupted, "nobody's going to have any cake until the judge here marries my brother and your sister. Then, we'll have turkey, cranberry sauce, and all the other fixings for Thanksgiving." She focused her violet eyes on the judge. "You know," she said, "with a little help from our moms and Grammy this afternoon, the two of them made all the food themselves."

That made sense, Judge Ingram thought. During the pre-wedding conference, the couple, clutching hands, told him they'd met in culinary school. "But for the top of her pressure cooker sticking, our paths never would have crossed."

"He unstuck it, and we've been together ever since." The bride-to-be squeezed her fiancé's hand and gave him the goofy look young couples often exchanged until the judge started raising the hard questions about their future life together.

"Judge," Pigtails said. She was going to be a looker he thought, watching her push a pigtail back with a slender hand. "Mama and Grammy want everything to go just right."

"I do, too." Judge Ingram busied himself readying the things he needed for the wedding. He checked that the page he planned to read from his bible was correctly bookmarked, the unity candle was ready to be lit, and the script he'd personalized for the wedding was tucked into his little black notebook. Running the correct pronunciation of the family names through his head, he wondered what the children's families thought about the upcoming nuptials.

He knew they couldn't be thrilled or one of their regular clergy would be officiating. Nobody requested the services of the "Go-to-Judge," as he fancied himself, unless there was a family problem or it was a mixed marriage. His scripts normally satisfied everyone by incorporating traditions from all faiths while sprinkling in enough passages from the Old and New Testaments to make the different factions feel comfortable. Most of the time, he figured, neither side realized the service wasn't slanted to either faith.

Turning back to the children, the judge saw that the four rows of folding chairs, separated by a center aisle, were beginning to fill. A number of the men on the groom's side were sporting button down shirts and a few baseball caps they'd yet to take off while the men on the bride's side uniformly wore blue blazers and grey slacks.

Judge Ingram glanced at his watch and told the children that it was time to spur the budding chefs to the altar. As he walked down the aisle to the kitchen, he couldn't help but calculate that there were only thirty-two chairs, an underwhelming number considering how large both families were.

The sound of something backfiring or exploding from the kitchen area interfered with his mathematics. His first instinct was to cower behind the two children, but since they were already running in the direction of the noise, he followed them.

The kitchen was quiet. The two mothers and grandmother stood silently on the far side of the island staring at the floor. From Judge Ingram's vantage point nothing seemed to be out of place. He moved closer to the sideboard where an entire feast of Thanksgiving fixings was set out buffet style for after the wedding.

Two gorgeous browned turkeys ringed by small potatoes sat on identical platters. Next to them, Judge Ingram could see into a bowl of green beans still bubbling with little French fried onions on top. He looked around for something that didn't seem right, noting gravy boats, plates with sliced jellied cranberry sauce, and yam casseroles with and without marshmallows. Three cooling pumpkin pies and a small wedding cake were on a side counter on the far side of the kitchen.

He paused, hearing whimpering but uncertain of its origin. The children had no doubts. They scurried toward the kitchen's center island but their tear-stained faced mothers moved quickly to prevent them from rounding its edge. Tommy's mother held him back by his arm and Melinda's mother engulfed her in a hug. The mothers left just enough room for Judge Ingram to slip by them, avoiding the yellow goop smeared across the end of the island that dripped onto the otherwise pristine floor.

The judge stopped short at the sight of the bride-to-be sitting with her back to the island cradling her groom-to-be. A shard of glass shaped like an icicle was sticking from the young man's chest. Judge Ingram glanced back at the mothers and ahead at Grammy and then stepped carefully toward the couple, avoiding the red and yellow mixture pooling on the linoleum floor. He reached forward to see if the groom-to-be still had a pulse.

Getting out of his way, the bride-to-be released one hand from her intended and gestured around the room at the splattered contents of what had been in the glass dish. "Corn puddin'," she said between sobs.

Judge Ingram quickly knew there wasn't going to be a wedding today or any other day. He straightened up, trying to calculate the odds of a man being impaled to death by a flying piece from a casserole dish, but it was too mind-boggling.

"Corn pudding?" he said.

"He didn't think my recipe was natural enough," the bride-to be said.

"So you killed him?"

"Oh no!" She clutched the silent groom closer to her.

"It was an accident," her mother said, releasing Tommy from her grasp. "An accident right after she took the corn puddin' out of the oven."

"I don't understand," Ingram said. He looked at the groom-to-be's mother, her face still buried in Melinda's corn silk hair and at Grammy, who, fists clenched, shook her head but remained silent.

"The rest of us were looking in the other direction putting the food out when my daughter stuck her mitted hands into the oven and transferred the corn puddin' from the oven to the counter." She nodded at her daughter encouraging her to pick up the tale.

The girl held her intended closer but, between sobs, continued. "Like Mama said, almost everything was ready so our moms and his Grammy were setting up the buffet. I was putting a garnish on the corn puddin' when he came around the island, nibbled my ear and decided to steal a taste."

She paused and looked up at Judge Ingram. "I usually make sweet things like the wedding cake. He specialized in savory dishes." She smoothed her intended's brow, leaving a dab of red on his forehead. "Even with our mothers and his Grammy helping today, we all had so much to get ready that I made the corn puddin'. I was supposed to use his grandmother's recipe, but I didn't have time."

Judge Ingram waited for her to go on. No sense rushing her. There would be enough commotion once the police came and the guests were told why the wedding was being cancelled.

"He took a bite, screwed up his face, and then spit it right back into the casserole dish. 'Trash absolute trash,' he yelled while he tried to throw my casserole into the garbage can."

"But it didn't end up in the garbage can?"

"No," she said. "I called him some choice names and grabbed the dish back from him."

"You struggled?"

Before she could respond, her mother said, "We all did."

"Excuse me?"

Melinda's mother raised her head. "Our backs were to our children when we heard them yapping at each other, but once we realized they were physically fighting over the casserole dish, the three of us jumped in to break things up."

Grammy unclenched her right fist and held it up so Judge Ingram could see her red and white blistered palm. "I got my hand on the corn puddin' dish, but it was too hot for me to hold."

"When she dropped it," the bride-to-be said, "it shattered against the island and I picked up a piece of the broken glass and ..."

"I yanked the shard away from my daughter, but it slipped from my hand. This is my fault." She leaned forward, but Judge Ingram stopped her before she touched the knifelike piece of glass.

He couldn't help but compare the trajectory of the shard and the blood splatter pattern on the bride-to-be's shirt and hands. Even without a protractor, there was no question in his mind that something didn't add up. He knew he should get on with calling the police and an ambulance, but he felt a need to learn more before the authorities muddied up the situation.

There obviously had to be some extenuating circumstances. He wondered if she would continue claiming her fiancé's death was an accident or switch to self-defense. At the very worst, surely a good attorney could cop a manslaughter plea on her behalf. Of course, Ingram realized, he would have to recuse himself from the case if it ended up on his docket. He cleared his throat. "You were saying."

Rather than answer, she began to cry again.

The pig-tailed little girl wiggled out of her mother's hug and planted herself between Judge Ingram and the couple on the floor. "You haven't answered the most important question. What did my brother think was wrong with the corn puddin'? What could be this wrong?" She pointed at her brother and then crossed her arms and waited for an answer.

The bride-to be kept her eyes lowered and muttered, "He didn't like my corn."

"Your corn?" Judge Ingram was confused. This was sounding less like a legal defense with everything she said.

"It was canned corn."

"You used canned corn for your own wedding corn puddin'?" Pigtails' face flushed as she swung her head from the couple on the floor to her grandmother's lined face. "For Grammy's corn puddin'?"

Judge Ingram tried to grasp why Pigtails was reacting more to the words "canned corn" than to the position her brother was in. "Don't you use canned corn in corn pudding?"

"Not if you're a real cook," Pigtails said. The bride wailed again. "The recipe for Thanksgiving Corn Puddin' like Grammy makes takes fresh corn kernels, eggs, real butter, honest to goodness sugar, salt, pepper, nutmeg and milk. Grammy usually adds a drop of sweet corn shine, too."

Pigtails shifted her eyes from Judge Ingram to the crying bride and then reached a finger out to the goop on the island. She licked her finger and immediately spit the pudding into the garbage can.

"Grammy taught us a real cook never uses anything but God's given ingredients. A real cook doesn't take short cuts. Grammy would have murdered my brother if he served anything with canned whole kernel corn and cream-style corn." She bent her head closer to the woman who would have been her sister-in-law. "I wouldn't be surprised if Grammy doesn't consider killing you, too."

The bride cried louder. She was still sobbing when the police led her away followed by her protesting mother. Her younger brother stood by the now unneeded wedding cake licking icing off his fingers.

* * *

Eighteen years later, newly retired Judge Ingram picked up one of the food magazines his wife kept stacked on the table between their two recliners. As he read the magazine's headline, about "Today's Hottest TV Chefs," the details of the corn puddin' wedding came back to him. He stared at the two pictures divided under the banner by a lightning bolt. The first, captioned "Cake King Tommy Hatfield," showed a dimple-cheeked chef behind a wedding cake waving his white icing covered fingers in the air. The other picture identified the woman with flowing auburn hair and violet eyes holding her signature corn puddin' casserole as "Melinda McCoy—from farm to table."

* * *

This was my second attempt to write a Thanksgiving story for the Untreed Reads Killer Wore Cranberry series. Although rejected, it was accepted and published by Kings River Life Magazine. A modified reprint, renamed Thanksgiving: I Do, I Don't, was included in Cooked to Death Vol. 4: COLD CUT FILES (March 14, 2019).

Legal Magic

*There are different types of sinfulness. Sometimes, it
is better to act and then ask forgiveness.*

In my book, keying a Mercedes because you think its eighty-plus-year-old owner is a Nazi meets the definition of malicious mischief, but explain that to my mother's Mah Jongg group. They are convinced that a Bunker & Davis attorney should be able to find a loophole even if there is—willful destruction of personal property, from actual ill will or resentment towards it owner.

"Stephen, the policeman who arrested Hannah must hate his own mother." Mrs. Berger hands me a piece of her chocolate marble cake. Unlike my mother who specializes in store bought, Mrs. Berger has been baking this same cake every fifth week for almost forty years. That's like four hundred marble cakes Karen Berger, Hannah Schwartz, Ella Goldring, and my mother have shared. Today, they watch me inhale Mrs. Berger's cake while their ivory tiles sit boxed on the floor of the Sunshine Retirement Village's cardroom.

"You need to call someone," Mrs. Berger instructs.

"Well," I start to respond to Mrs. Berger, who, while not quite five feet tall, has the most authoritative voice and demeanor I have ever encountered in my life, but Mrs. Goldring interrupts. Mrs. Goldring's doctor attributes diminished impulse control to her last stroke, but mother claims 'Ella always wandered between the present and past as long as the topic was 'me,' 'me,' 'me.'

"Maybe you could call Judge Holly and explain this silly misunderstanding," Mrs. Goldring says. She peers over her reading glasses at the piece of paper entitled Notice of Hearing. Pausing to push a straying strand of grey hair back behind her ear, she continues: "Girls, you remember how nice Judge Holly was when he spoke to garden club? Surely Stephen, you can convince him Hannah shouldn't be punished."

Fat chance. They say a good lawyer knows the law while a better lawyer knows the judge. I only appeared in front of him once, but I know Judge Holly is a snake. If I take the case, which I don't want to do, I will be lucky to get Hannah Schwartz off with a slapped wrist, restitution, and maybe, only because of being seventy-three, community service. Judge Holly was kinder and gentler while on the re-election circuit, but only because he knew if he got beat he couldn't qualify for a pension.

Clearing my throat, I explain the law to these women whose faces I know so well. No go. They believe keying a Mercedes from front to back is understandable, not a criminal act. Ignoring mother, I try again. "A criminal lawyer would know Judge Holly better …."

I can feel the look my mother is giving me. There will be no palming off of this case. What can I do? Jewish guilt is a wonderful tool. My mother has known how to use it since I can remember. I think that's why I became a lawyer. So she couldn't have the joy, while flicking an ivory tile with a long pink nail the exact shade of her hair, to brag about "My son, the doctor."

Like Mrs. Berger, who sometimes brags on her son, the veterinarian, my mom takes credit for having raised a professional. While close, it doesn't count. The only one who can boast a medical doctor is Mrs. Schwartz, but she never does. He married a non-Jew.

At least I did that right. My wife, Jennifer, and I were in Hebrew school carpool together. We both have stereotypical curly dark hair and brown eyes, but at six two and 210 pounds, I'm no Woody Allen, and Jen cleans up well, too. Our daughter, Molly, is six, but with thick wavy brown hair, charcoal eyes, and a nose to die for. I'm already trying to figure out how to keep our doors locked.

My mother takes credit for Molly's good looks. If I point out that Molly doesn't resemble her, she reminds me that if she hadn't married by dearly departed father, Molly's hair and nose wouldn't be in our family.

These women trust the head of BD's collections department, who finished in the top ten percent of his class, to craft a winning defense strategy. They don't realize I'm the only attorney sitting in a basement with thirty women who spend every day threatening people to pay up money they owe. It isn't glamorous, but the firm is happy with the department's profitability so I'm sure I can stay on the non-partnership track.

"I have appeared in front of him and while I can't call the judge, if you want, Mrs. Schwartz, I would be honored to represent you."

"Thank you, Stephen." Mrs. Schwartz responds in heavily accented English. "You make Kimbleski rot in hell."

"Whoa, we're trying to get you off. Punishing him isn't on our agenda. Our problem is you keyed Mr. Kimble's car while he watched."

"Kimbleski," mother corrects. "He was a guard at Dachau when Hannah was there." Mother reaches across the couch and takes one of the blue veined hands lying in Mrs. Schwartz's lap. Gently pulling it to her, mother turns it over and pushes Mrs. Schwartz's trademark long sleeve up so that I can see the number tattooed on her wrist. "Tell him," mother encourages.

"I tried to tell the policeman that Kimble wasn't his name, but he wouldn't listen to me. I pointed out the scar on his shoulder, but the policeman mumbled 'men often have scars or tattoos you'd never expect to see under their shirts' when he took the key out of my hand."

"We thought the officer was going to show us something under his shirt, but he just guided her into his car and said he was 'arresting her for malicious mischief,'" Mother says. "I tried to ride with her, but that rotten pig wouldn't let me. I had to drive my own car to bail Hannah out."

I can imagine what the cop was thinking when he looked from a perfectly toned octogenarian staring at his damaged Mercedes to four angry women with sagging chins, over-made up faces, and hair colors that range from pink to blue-grey. I would have arrested the one with the key in her hand, too.

"Don't jump to conclusions," mother reproves me. "She was justified. Kimbleski is a Nazi."

"A Nazi," Mrs. Goldring repeats loudly, as if I haven't heard the first few times. All my legal instincts and gut feelings know this isn't a legal defense, but looking at the stillness with which Mrs. Schwartz holds her exposed arm, I listen.

"I remember him. His voice, eyes, scar." For a minute, I think she is pulling a Mrs. Goldring. "When I saw him hosing his car, I blurted out, 'Commandant Kimbleski.' He turned, almost hitting me with the water, and said, 'My name is Kimble.'"

"Why didn't you just let it be? Maybe call the Weisenthal group who track war criminals? Why key his car?"

"So the police would come."

Now, I understand. Mrs. Schwartz believed a policeman on her word would arrest Kimble. Instead, the young officer assumed, especially with the key still in her hand, that Mrs. Schwartz was the one to lock-up.

"After your mother left, I tried to talk to Mr. Kimble. He ignored me and just kept trying to wash the key mark off his car," Mrs. Berger said.

"I don't know if we can wash this case away. Mrs. Schwartz, even with your reasons, keying a car is malicious mischief."

"Stephen!"

"But I hope to find a way around it." Mother smiles.

* * *

As I've said before, Judge Holly is not a jovial jurist. His claim to fame dates back to a neck injury eight years ago. Until he had surgery, he heard cases lying on a cot behind his bench. It kept his docket from backing up, but I can't tell you how disturbing it was trying a case to an unseen judge.

Judge Holly is sitting up again, but he doesn't tolerate fools or foolish cases. For today's pre-trial conference, I fit both categories. Not only does my client meet the technical requirements of the alleged crime, but I've filed a creative cross-complaint hoping for a settlement. Unfortunately, Erica Stern, Kimble's attorney, doesn't believe in settling. She argues that with all due respect to the defendant's past, there can be no reasonable belief of fear of assault from a garden hose.

"Ms. Stern, I understand your position, but before we proceed, I suggest," Judge Holly says looking straight at me, "that the two of you go have a cup of coffee."

I barely place the two cups of black coffee I bought in the snack bar on the table, when Erica makes it clear that the only way she'll settle is full restitution, formal apology, and withdraw the assault charge.

"I can't agree to that." My mother would kill me. I wish I could make everything about this case disappear, but I never got too far learning magic. I couldn't do simple card tricks let alone pulling rabbits out of hats. "It seems to me that the first thing we need to determine is if Mr. Kimble has standing."

"What?"

"If Kimble is actually Kimbleski, as Mrs. Schwartz believes, there is no case. He should be turned over to INS for deportation. Perhaps you should advise your client of our position?"

Erica Stern has an ethical duty to talk to her client before we tell Judge Holly that we have reached an impasse. She wanders down the hall towards the pay phones, but comes back so quickly that I know she made as much contact with her client as I made with mine before refusing the settlement offer. We return to Judge Holly's chambers to find he left but that if we were unable to settle; we must return tomorrow at nine.

Back at my office, I look at my billing sheet. Maybe, I can justify Mrs. Schwartz' case as pro bono. Somehow, I don't think BD would be happy with my association with this case. Putting the timesheet down, I try earning real billables. I dictate a few Mae West letters, the kind inviting you to come see me with payment within ten days. My phone rings: Erica Stern. No pleasantries.

"I talked to Mr. Kimble again. He is dismayed at the anguish he apparently has caused Mrs. Schwartz."

"Excuse me?" She ignores me. "Because he is an immigrant, he is sensitive to the emotions that triggered this situation. He didn't know why she keyed his car, but now he has no desire to upset her further."

"So?"

"So, Mr. Kimble, having considered everything, especially the age of everyone involved, proposes an offer that while I'm not fully in agreement with, he insists I tender."

"I'm listening."

"Mr. Kimble took a short term lease at Sunshine while handling some business in Atlanta."

We've hit a nerve. The only short term leases at Sunshine are caused by death. "He plans to move this weekend. Consequently, rather than returning for trial and to spare Mrs. Schwartz, all claims dropped and no further action."

"The Mercedes?"

"A simple paint job that he will take care of."

"His status in this country?"

"Status quo."

"Where is he moving?"

"I'm not at liberty to say."

"I'll run it by my client. Considering the fear and memories that Kimbleski generated in her, I'm not sure she is going to be willing to settle without monetary compensation." I pause, hoping Erica Stern will offer more, but she doesn't. Telling her I will get back to her, I hang up and yell "YES!" Then, I call and explain the offer to Mrs. Schwartz.

"Whatever you say, Stephen. You're my lawyer."

I admonish her not to hit the tops off parking meters with a baseball bat. She has no idea what I'm talking about, but tells me what a good boy I am.

After formally accepting the offer, I dummy a few hours to cover my creative practice of law. Then, I think how mother is going to sound at the next few Mah Jongg games talking about "my son, the lawyer.

* * *

An earlier version of Legal Magic, Malicious Mischief won a 2010 Chattahoochee Valley Writers Conference Short Story Award in 2010. Reworked as Legal Magic, the story received an Alabama Writers Conclave Humor Award in 2011. When published in the 2011 Alalit, it became my first published short story. I enjoyed Michael and the Mah Jongg Players so much that I later included them in my novel, Should Have Played Poker: a Carrie Martin and the Mah Jongg Players Mystery.

This is Where I Buried My Wives

"This is where I buried my wives," Biff said. He stared beyond the two marked graves down the hill at the orchard and lush pasture that divided the land between a few worn chicken houses and the newly fenced horse ring that abutted the main house.

"Present company excepted, I hope."

"I certainly hope so." He drew Julie closer to him with the arm that wasn't carrying their picnic basket. "To me, this is the prettiest spot on the farm. I know it may seem morbid, but I come up here when I need to think or bounce an idea off someone. There aren't a lot of people in these parts and sometimes I just need to talk things out."

Julie raised her head and kissed his rough cheek. "You won't have to talk to the dead anymore. You've got me now."

She took the picnic basket from his hand and bent down to smooth out their blanket, positioning it so their backs would be to the graves. She pulled some flowers from the basket and arranged them on the side of the blanket. As Julie set out napkins and utensils, she paused and looked up at the sky. "It feels like there should be a big tree shading this hill."

"There used to be a giant elm back there. Some disease got it right around the time Margie died." Biff plopped onto the blanket. He accommodated his six-foot frame by extending his booted legs onto the grass. Julie snuggled against him.

"Margie brought me up here shortly after we met." Biff hesitated. "It was her favorite place in the world, so it seemed only right to bury her on the hill. Besides, if it hadn't been for her leaving me all the land you can see between here and the main house," he said, pointing, "I'd still be living by those egg houses."

Julie's eyes followed his finger to the small parcel on which the chicken houses sat. It was definitely a tiny space compared with the rest of the farmland. She put her hand on his arm. "Was that the land your family owned?"

"No, we squatted on that small patch and were tenant farmers to Margie's grand-parents on the rest of it." He watched Julie's face. "Like I told you, Margie was married and lost her husband and daughter well before I came to work for her. She may have been getting on in years, but somehow we clicked. I like to think I made those last few years of her life happy."

"You're making my life pretty happy." Julie handed him a sandwich. "Turkey and parsnip." He made a face, but took the sandwich and bit into it.

"I want you to know everything," Biff said. "You're going to hear people say some mean things like Margie was old enough to be my mother and …"

Julie hushed him by pressing her hand against his lips. "I won't listen to them as long as you don't pay attention if someone talks about me being eighteen years younger than you."

"Heck, I'm proud to have a trophy wife." Biff grinned and hugged her. "Just so you know, I never asked for this farm. I was as shocked as anyone when I found out Margie left it to me. "He glanced behind him. "I buried her up here because she loved this place."

"It probably also reminds you of how far you've come." Julie noticed that the smile lingered on Biff's lips, but was no longer in his eyes. She quickly added, "Not to mention how lonely having this big a farm must have been without someone to share it with. I'm so glad you decided to take another chance on FarmDatesR4U."

"Me, too." He raised his shoulders and turned his head toward the second grave marker. "I almost didn't. After Annie and I got together, I didn't think I could ever be happier. I can't begin to tell you how thrilled I was to find a city slicker willing to give up the big city for life on my farm. When our time together turned out to be so short, I was scared to try again." He finished his sandwich and sidled closer to Julie.

"You don't ever have to worry," she said. "I may only have spent a few summers on my grandparents' farm, but the experience ruined me from ever being a pure city dweller. I can remember riding my granddad's tractor as he did the planting, feeding slop to the pigs, rocking on the porch at night with granny, and best of all climbing a tree like the elm you told me was here. I'd sit in the crook of that tree, looking out as far as I could see, unaware of how perfect my world was." She kissed him again. "Thank you for giving me my farm life back."

Biff leaned back on his hands. "What happened to your grandparents' farm? Did they sell it?"

Julie turned to rummage in the picnic basket. She pulled out a tin with dessert in it. "Apple pie?" She cut Biff a large slice.

"You didn't answer me," he said, gobbling down the pie.

"Oh, there isn't much to tell. Like her mother before her, my mom had me when she was sixteen. Dad enlisted to pay their bills. Until she died when I was seven, we lived wherever the Army assigned him. After her death, Dad sent me to spend a few summers with my grandparents, but once he remarried, I went to boarding schools and camps. My grandfather died and somewhere along the way, my grandmother gave away the farm."

Julie brushed a crumb off Biff's shirt. "Like I've told you, try as I might, I wasn't meant for the bar scene, concrete sidewalks, and cars and people everywhere. A friend told me about FarmDatesR4U.com. I debated it for a few months, but as a twenty-sixth birthday present to myself I signed up for a two-week trial subscription. Your profile popped up on the thirteenth day." She waved her hand all around her. "And, as they say, the rest is history."

Biff tried to kiss her again, but she blocked his efforts by putting both hands on his chest. He sat back. "Biff, one thing we never talked about. Our relationship and marriage happened so quickly. I mean, it was only a matter of months between our first messages, your proposal and my moving out here for good." She paused before the words rushed out. "Your profile was online for a lot longer time than mine. Were there any other girls you dated?"

"A few."

She swallowed. "Were you serious with any of them? Did you bring any of them to this hill?"

He looked away from her toward a pile of rocks near the bottom of the hill. "You don't really want to go there."

"I do. I want to know." She moved away from him.

Biff ran his hand through his hair. "That's what Annie said. Why can't we simply be happy as we are?"

Julie pulled her knees close to her and put her arms around them. She tried to wait him out and finally said, "Biff, I need to know."

Biff again glanced at the pile of rocks and back at Julie. "A few came to the farm, but they weren't like Annie or you. Oh, they said the right things about being willing to try farm life. And, at first, they admired the wide-open spaces, the crops and animals, and the stream running through our property, but then they started complaining. They refused to help with the chores and couldn't appreciate the songs of the coyotes. One didn't like the smell of the egg houses, another refused to throw slop in the pig trough, and a third said planting in the sun wasn't good for her delicate skin. I realized pretty quickly that none of them would ever be able to earn a place on the top of this hill."

"So, they had to stay at the bottom?"

"That's right. I thought you were going to be different."

"Oh, I am," Julie said. "I'm not going to end up at the bottom of the hill."

"No, you're not." Biff stood and took a step toward her, but stumbled. He sat back down on the blanket and held his head. Julie inched a little further away from him as he attempted to stand again. He tried to focus his gaze on her. "Julie, what's going on?"

"Nothing a farm boy can't understand. You should have looked at the parsnip a little more closely. We city slickers sometimes confuse parsnip and hemlock. Sorry."

He reached for her, but missed. "You might want to lie still," Julie said, as he grabbed his stomach and doubled up from a wave of pain. Turning away from him, Julie took the cut flowers she had left on the blanket and walked up the hill toward the two graves. She placed all but one on Annie's grave before moving on to Margie's spot at the top of the hill.

Carefully, Julie knelt and put the remaining single white rose in front of the simple white marker. She ignored the sounds behind her, but spoke loudly enough that her words carried downhill. "I never stopped loving this farm or you, Granny. When Dad took me away, I told you I'd come home one day. I'm sorry I was too late, but I'm making up for it now. You don't have to worry, I've made sure the farm is back in the family."

* * *

Originally published by Bethlehem Writers Roundtable in September/October 2015, This is Where I Buried My Wives was reprinted by Tough magazine in August 2023.